RSVP FOR MURDER

A VIV VOGEL, WEDDING PLANNER COZY MYSTERY

C.J. LEE

CHAPTER 1

*V*ivian Vogel stood in the back of Marco's Little Italy restaurant, keeping a firm eye on the guests of the Giovanni family's wedding rehearsal dinner. She situated herself in the corner, asserting her presence without seeming to intrude on the party.

Cocktail hour had begun, and a large and lively throng shouted over the din, jostling for drinks at the bar. Minutes earlier, a small dust-up had broken out between the bride and her bridesmaid. Now, Sal Giovanni, the bride's father, was arguing with his uncle Gino.

Evidently, Gino Giovanni didn't appreciate the way his nephew was looking at him. Gino being halfway drunk already didn't help much, either. Viv was impressed with how much booze the old man could still knock back. Even though she sat Sal and Gino far apart at different tables, as instructed, they still found a way to get at each other.

Viv marveled at how relatively minor these issues were, given everything she had dealt with since agreeing to plan the wedding of Sal and Toni Giovanni's daughter, Shauna. Besides supervising the staff and keeping Toni reasonably satisfied, there wasn't much left for Viv to do tonight. She used this downtime to observe the crowd and do some people-watching.

Toni commanded the attention of several women who swarmed around her. Propping her phone nearby, she animatedly demonstrated some beauty products plucked from a shabby pink vinyl handbag, a stark contrast to her designer gown and flashy jewelry.

Toni addressed her hyped-up sales pitch to the phone's camera and her captive audience. Viv guessed she was live streaming this demonstration on MyFace, as Toni was apt to do.

Sal stood clustered with a group of men, talking in low, serious murmurs peppered with laughter. After their testy exchange, Viv observed Sal glancing at Uncle Gino, who was sitting with a small group at his assigned table, eating a bowl of minestrone and guzzling more wine. Viv sighed and shook her head — the soup wasn't to be served until the beginning of dinner. Gino must have convinced one of the staff to bring it to him from the kitchen.

AT LAST, cocktail hour was scheduled to end, and Viv walked over to ask the D.J. to pause the music and make the dinner announcement as soon as possible, before something else went wrong. The D.J. nodded, smiling at her approach, but before he could speak, a piercing scream punctured the room.

"Uncle Gino!" a woman wailed. "He's on the floor in front of the men's room — somebody help!"

More cries met Viv's ears as she followed a group of people running down the hall toward the restrooms. They discovered Gino sprawled on the floor, his legs akimbo and protruding into the hallway.

The door to the men's room was ajar and leaning against his body, prompting a concerned guest to rush over and pull him into the hall. Barely conscious, he was pale and taking shallow breaths, covered in sweat.

"Uncle Gino, what's wrong? Can you hear me?" the man asked, alarmed.

Gino blinked his eyes and lifted his head slightly, feverishly working his mouth, trying to speak. "Soooup," he managed to croak out before slumping back down, going still. Less than fifteen minutes later, Gino Giovanni, the figurehead of the Giovanni family, was pronounced dead.

CHAPTER 2

Nearly a year before this tragic event occurred, Viv awoke from a fitful night's sleep in her childhood home. The house, a recent unexpected inheritance from her mother, had come into her possession after her mother's abrupt departure to Marrakesh, Morocco to live with an antiquities dealer she hardly knew.

Rubbing her temples, Viv acknowledged Aggie, her black and white Australian shepherd mix, who was pawing at the door to be let outside. Aggie originally belonged to her mother and was another much-welcomed part of the inheritance.

Bleary-eyed, Viv glanced at the clock: 10:30 a.m. She blamed herself for staying up late again and trudged to let Aggie out. Sleep had been elusive lately; the house's creaks and groans unsettled her at night. Adjusting to life there again was proving difficult.

Viv brushed her teeth and splashed her face with cold water; the dark circles under her striking hazel eyes were plainly evident in the mirror, a visible reminder of her poor sleep habits. After a quick shower, she donned a simple black dress and flats, opting for no makeup and tying her long brown hair into a ponytail.

With a cup of coffee in hand, Viv stared out at the misty rain, still grappling with the reality of being back in her small hometown.

Harborside, Rhode Island, wasn't considerably far from her previous home in Manhattan. Although only about four and a half hours away, including the ferry ride, it couldn't be any farther apart from New York in terms of vibe or character.

Located on Manitou Island, Harborside had been famous for being the smallest town in the smallest state in the U.S., but more recently gained fame as a premier wedding destination spot.

A lot has changed since social media first ignited the weddings on Manitou. A number-one ranking in *New Bride* magazine and being featured on some notable wedding reality shows made Manitou an internationally renowned wedding destination, now unofficially known as "Wedding Island."

Boasting miles of picturesque shoreline, two lighthouses, and three quaint churches, it's the ideal setting for a unique wedding experience. The local scenery is picture-postcard perfect, complete with a white church on top of a grassy green hillside and wild roses blushing pink in the summer.

Now, in early November, with the froth of winter waves breaking against the tidal shoreline, the island slept peacefully and its nearly two thousand full-time residents were relieved to reclaim their tranquil paradise.

· · ·

Viv's BUSINESS line suddenly rang, snapping her out of her reverie. She fumbled to pick up the phone.

"Hello, Fabulously Ever After, Viv speaking."

Viv opened her wedding planning business, Fabulously Ever After, in September right at the tail end of the season. She runs her business out of the small mother-in-law's quarters behind her house, the perfect spot for an office space. So far, Viv only had two weddings scheduled for next summer, knowing she had to book more if her fledgling business was going to survive.

"Hi Viv, this is Libby Greene. I'm an assistant to Antonia Giovanni and speaking on her behalf." The young woman's voice was hurried and shaky, hinting at some distress.

"Hello Libby, what can I do for you and Ms. Giovanni? Is she planning on getting married?"

"Well, it's *Mrs.* Giovanni. Her daughter Shauna is getting married and wants her wedding to take place on Manitou Island after watching the episode of *Monster Brides* that was filmed there. Toni would like to hire someone local to help plan everything."

"Well, you've come to the right place! Have they set a date for the wedding yet?"

"Not an exact date, but they were thinking the first weekend after Labor Day in September?"

"Okay, let me take a peek at my calendar for that weekend."

Viv knew full well she didn't have any weddings booked for next September, but didn't want to appear *too* free.

She came back on after a minute, chirping, "Yes, that week looks good. Once we have the location figured out I'll check on availability and we can nail down the date. Do they have a spot in mind for the ceremony?"

"That hasn't been discussed yet, as Shauna's engagement was just announced today. She and Toni would like to meet you in person and check things out. Does January tenth at noon work for you?"

"Let's see… ah yes, I am free that day."

"That's great news," Libby sighed with relief. "Toni will be pleased. She's the one handling all the wedding details, and she has very high standards, just a heads up," Libby warned, lowering her voice. "But it probably will be a lucrative opportunity for you as the Giovannis have a large social circle and are willing to spend a lot on this event."

"Well, I'm definitely up for the task."

Viv then heard a commotion of a woman yelling in the background on the other end of the line.

"Can you please hold on for one second?"

Viv could hear part of Libby's muffled conversation where she had set the phone down.

"But I swear I've looked everywhere and just can't find designer silk pajamas for dogs. I'm sorry!" Viv heard Libby pleading to someone. *"Yeah… yes m'am, of course, I will call a tailor right away."*

Picking up the phone again, a rattled Libby said to Viv, "Sorry about that. I'm back."

"Is everything okay there?"

"Yes… I'm… it's fine," Libby stammered. "I gotta go. They'll be there for the appointment in January. Good luck to you."

The line went dead as Libby abruptly hung up.

Viv wondered at the oddness of this encounter and what it meant regarding her potential new clients. She was uncertain about the Giovannis' actual commitment to coming in January, given the rush and lack of pertinent questions from their assistant — namely about Viv's fee and other important details that most clients want to know immediately.

By LATER THAT afternoon the brisk autumn day had cleared up, so Viv decided to head down to Barb's Bakery and see her sister Betsy. Since returning home she visited with her older and only sibling almost daily. Viv couldn't wait to tell Betsy about this new prospective opportunity — she needed as much business as possible to preserve her dwindling savings account.

As Viv walked the empty cobblestone streets, the crisp breeze brushed her cheeks and whipped her hair around her face, pushing the fallen leaves on the sidewalks into swirling eddies. She breathed in the sharp smell of old leaves mixed with the sea air, lost in her thoughts.

CHAPTER 3

Six months ago, Viv couldn't have imagined this life. She had been content as a project manager at a tech startup in New York, living in her modest Manhattan condo. At thirty-four, she reveled in the carefree single life, surrounded by friends.

Then came the unexpected news like a thunderbolt: her mother, Barbara, had fallen for Alastair, a wealthy British antiquities dealer living in Marrakesh. He was visiting Manitou Island; they met by chance one day, keeping their connection going after he returned to Morocco. Alastair convinced Barb to leave everything behind — including her beloved bakery and home, urging her to join him.

Viv hurried back to Harborside to address this brewing family crisis. She and Betsy tried to dissuade their mother from making such a drastic move with a man she had known for only a few months. However, their sensible concerns fell on deaf ears.

Widowed for nearly a decade, Barb yearned for adventure and was ready to take the leap. She assured her daughters she would be fine and offered the bakery to Betsy and the house to Viv. Despite their reservations, Barb's mind was made up. After her retirement party and farewell festivities, Viv returned to New York over Betsy's objections.

Back in the city while at the grocery store checkout, Viv spotted an issue of *New Bride* magazine featuring a smiling couple on Manitou Island's beach. "Find Out Our Top Picks For Your Destination Wedding Bliss!" the headline blared. Rolling her eyes, she impulsively tossed it into her cart, struck by sudden inspiration.

Inheriting her mother's house left Viv with three choices: either sell it, rent it out, or move back to Harborside and live in it. Viv didn't want to sell the house she and Betsy grew up in nor deal with the hassle of renting to strangers. The sprawling two-story New England farmhouse with its vast enclosed sunroom and small cottage near prime beachfront property could fetch a good price — but she couldn't bear the thought.

And what about work? Viv couldn't see herself at her mother's bakery like Betsy; baking wasn't her forte. Burned scones and underdone cakes marked her teenage years of helping at the bakery.

Wedding planning wasn't new to Viv. As a top-notch project manager, she had jumped at the chance to help when a friend got married three years earlier. Word spread, and she soon found herself helping several more friends and co-workers to coordinate their weddings.

Those lavish city ceremonies went off without a hitch, leaving everyone happy. Handling demanding clients and unforeseen crises was second nature to Viv, and she easily established connections with vendors, which was essential in the wedding business.

The magazine article felt like a sign. Her hometown was becoming a wedding hotspot! With a house waiting for her and plenty of room for an office, why not start her own wedding-planning business? Surely there was a demand on the island now. And Betsy never stopped asking when she would leave the "rat race" behind and move back home.

So Viv set her plan into motion, jumping into the unknown and the uncertainties of undertaking a brand new enterprise. And back to where she grew up, in a town where everyone knows everyone else's business. The people are friendly and helpful, though sometimes it feels like living under a microscope.

If her business failed, she couldn't simply run away from everything. Plus, she had somehow underestimated the monotony and predictability of her hometown; adjusting to the slower pace would take some effort after being immersed in the breakneck speed of city life for so long.

AFTER ABOUT TWENTY minutes of walking in the fresh autumn air, Viv finally arrived at her familial haven, Barb's Bakery. The venerable shop had scarcely changed since their mother opened it over thirty years ago. The steadfast red brick exterior had withstood the relentless march of time, and a charming blue and white striped awning, though faded from decades under the sun's scrutiny, reached out like a guardian over the entrance. The bakery's moniker was boldly declared in an eye-catching shade of crimson arched across a vast window that spanned nearly the entire wall, filling the shop with daylight.

A formidable counter commanded attention on one side of the shop; its age-etched wooden surface bore silent testimony to its former existence as a general store counter where customers would have once relayed their shopping needs to an obliging attendant to fetch their goods. Now, it had been converted into a showcase and hosted an enticing spectacle — tiers upon tiers of freshly baked delicacies.

An operational antique cash register held court at one end, its polished brass surface gleaming under the warm illumination of suspended Edison bulbs, which cast an inviting amber glow across the room. Behind this time-honored artifact lay a sizable storeroom that had been ingeniously transformed into an impressive commercial kitchen.

The shop fit eight small tables comfortably, each draped with vintage floral tablecloths while mismatched ceramic mugs added to the quirky decor. Walls adorned with framed black-and-white photographs narrated tales from another era, adding to this tapestry woven with nostalgia and community spirit. Barb's was the go-to spot where locals liked to gather early mornings and Sundays after church for coffee, pastries, and a healthy dose of the latest gossip.

"Hey sis," Betsy greeted Viv as she walked in. The glass-windowed door was affixed with a bell but was hardly necessary as the ancient wooden floorboards creaked loudly enough to signal a patron's entry. "Want a croissant? I just finished a batch and they're still warm."

Betsy had lived in Harborside for most of her life, only leaving home to attend college in Pennsylvania. She returned six years later with her fiancé Jake in tow, somehow convincing him to move from Philly to the middle of nowhere. At that time, Viv and Betsy's mother needed help running her shop. Betsy herself was a fantastic baker, so naturally she volunteered to come back and help. Being a more domestic type than Viv, she didn't mind settling down and raising a family on the island.

Now married to Jake and with two young kids, Betsy was the new proprietor of Barb's Bakery. Barb was so well-regarded as a lifelong resident of Harborside, Betsy wouldn't ever dream of changing the name. She had watched her mother carefully make all the croissants, cakes, and pastries for years and had learned from her.

She learned about the importance of fresh ingredients, the value of taking care to cut the butter into the flour just so, kneading the dough until it was silky smooth. Betsy was able to maintain the bakery's reputation for quality with ease and kept the loyal customers coming back.

Viv helped herself to a croissant and took a seat. A masterful perfection of flakiness, the warm burst of buttery goodness made her want to grab another, but thought twice. She was trying to eat healthier and avoid stress eating. The temptations of the bakery were too much sometimes.

"So, how's business these days?" Betsy inquired.

Viv proceeded to tell her about the strange phone call with Libby Greene, the harried assistant of *Mrs.* Antonia Giovanni.

"Oh jeez, Viv. You might wanna watch out for these folks. Throwing a fit over designer silk dog pajamas? Talk about a red flag alert."

Viv laughed in agreement. "We'll see, but I'm not in

much of a position to turn down any clients these days. Toni and her daughter are coming for an initial appointment in January, although I'm half expecting them to cancel. And if you're lucky, you'll get to make the wedding cake," she added playfully.

"Wow, can't wait," Betsy deadpanned. "Hey, I've been meaning to ask, did you decide what you're doing for Thanksgiving yet? Can I talk you out of going to the city this year?"

For the past few years, Viv had alternated between spending Thanksgiving with her friends in New York and her family back home in Harborside. This year, she had intended to spend the holiday with her old friends but was having second thoughts since this would be the first Thanksgiving since their mother ran off to Marrakesh and Viv didn't want to leave her sister.

"Yeah Betsy, I think I'll probably stay here this time," Viv said with a sigh.

"That's great! I'm so glad that you're coming. And we've got some special guests," Betsy teased. "Wanna guess who?"

Viv's face blanched as she realized whom Betsy was talking about. "No, Betsy! Why?"

Betsy let out a little chuckle. "Don't be selfish, Vivian! This is Max's first Thanksgiving with Lizzy since Emily left him. There's no reason for the two of them to be alone for the holiday. Jake and I have plenty of room at our place. The more, the merrier!" she added with a wry smile.

Viv's THOUGHTS drifted to the night she showed up at her mother's going away party a few months earlier and immediately spotted Maxwell Bennett, Manitou Island's deputy sheriff, and her ex-boyfriend from high school. As a good friend of Betsy's husband, Jake, Max was invited to the celebration. Viv felt a twinge of bittersweet nostalgia as she watched him from across the room.

When they were young, he broke her heart by dumping her for her best friend, Emily. Of course, her friendship with Emily ended then as well. Max and Emily eventually married, and they now have a ten-year-old daughter named Lizzy. But two years ago, Emily suddenly left Max for another man she met online, leaving him devastated and alone.

Despite their history, Viv found herself having a long conversation with Max, where she agreed to meet with him sometime "just for coffee." She took him up on the offer shortly after moving back to town. Their coffee date turned into drinks and dinner at the Harborside Cafe.

While they caught up on each other's lives, Viv couldn't help but admire how young and fit Max still looked, albeit with a bit of a paunchier waistline and some gray evident in the stubble on his face. At just over six feet tall with broad shoulders, hair the color of rich espresso, and piercing blue eyes, he was considered the most eligible bachelor in Harborside, not to mention the subject of frequent gossip.

Max wore a plaid flannel shirt, faded jeans, and brown suede work-style boots for their casual date. Viv felt a little overdressed in comparison, wearing a forest-green silk blouse and black slacks, but Max was very neatly put together, with an enticing hint of musky cologne wafting over to her side of the table. When he rolled up his sleeves, she observed a tattoo featuring stylized numbers in a delicate script on the back of his left forearm. When Viv inquired, Max informed her it was the date of his daughter's birth — the best day of his life.

As the night went on, Max made a confession that surprised Viv: he regretted breaking up with her in high school and wished he hadn't married Emily. However, Viv couldn't bring herself to believe him — it seemed like he was only saying these things because his wife had cheated on him and left.

Feeling annoyed by his surely insincere admission, Viv made an excuse about having an early day and went home. After that night, she swore to herself that she wouldn't let Max get close to her again, ignoring his calls and texts afterward.

AND NOW BETSY dared to invite him to their family's Thanksgiving dinner! Ever since Viv moved back to Harborside, Betsy had been champing at the bit to get Viv and Max back together.

"I know what you're trying to do. Can't we just leave the past alone?" Viv asked her sister, exasperated.

"But he's so cute! And a great father — have you seen how much he adores Lizzy? I know he likes you. Do you want to stay single forever?"

"Yeah, he likes me now that Emily's out of the picture," Viv replied sullenly. "Look, I appreciate that you think you're being helpful, but please stop trying to set us up. I never should have gone out with him when I first came back. I just don't feel like I can trust him yet. I'll still come to Thanksgiving, but I swear if you try to seat me next to him, I'll remove myself to the kiddie's table."

"Alright. No more, I promise," Betsy responded, quickly crossing her fingers behind her back.

Viv finished her coffee and started for the door. "Well, I've got work to do."

"Hey Viv," Betsy called out after her. "Don't be mad. Max really is a great guy. He told me how terrible he felt about what happened in high school. He was just young and dumb. I wish you'd give him a chance."

"Okay, I get it. But seriously, no way."

Secretly, Viv didn't want to admit that deep down she was beginning to develop feelings for Max again. The truth was, they mostly had a great time when they went out a few months ago. But she was in a vulnerable place, uprooting herself from life in the city and dealing with her mother's abrupt departure halfway across the world.

And Viv knew she had to protect herself — she was all too aware of how falling in love with someone could end up. In fact, just a couple of years ago, she ended an engagement to her ex-boyfriend after she discovered that he was cheating on her.

These past experiences of heartbreak had taught Viv to protect her emotions diligently. She learned to build strong barriers around her heart, ensuring that it remained safe from the uncertainties of love.

Viv paused to take in the magnificent view of the shoreline as she walked back from the bakery. While gazing at the steel-gray water of the receding tide, she observed a shooting star in the faint eastern twilight. She couldn't resist making a wish, a habit she had held onto since childhood.

Viv wished that something exciting would happen in her life. She desperately hoped that she wouldn't regret trading the skyscrapers of Manhattan for seashells on the beach.

CHAPTER 4

$\mathcal{V}$iv managed to survive the holidays mostly unscathed, and on a chilly Tuesday morning in early January she was in her office behind the main house doing some last-minute straightening up.

She had recently finished renovating and decorating her office, putting more time and effort into it than the house itself. Viv thought it was important to give the right impression to clients and spent hours picking out the furnishings and decor. She settled on a tasteful and simple mid-century modern look, in a palette of muted grays and turquoise blue. Her favorite touch was the round vintage fish eye mirror on the far wall, which she found in a local antique store.

Viv checked the time on her phone. The Giovannis were running late for their consultation appointment. To her amazement, they didn't end up canceling the meeting after all. She was both apprehensive and also genuinely curious to meet them. Viv reminded herself that she had handled many difficult clients throughout her former career, and the key was to manage expectations from the start. Although gauging from her conversation with Toni's assistant, she could only imagine what their expectations might be.

Viv's phone dinged — a text from Toni Giovanni.

> So sorry hun, missed ferry. Caught next one, see u in a couple hours. Hope is ok. Toni xoxo

ABOUT TWO AND a half hours later, a large black SUV pulled into the driveway. A woman with short dark hair streaked with brassy highlights and layers that dramatically flipped upwards got out of the passenger side, talking and gesturing to the driver holding the door open.

With oversized rhinestone studded sunglasses perched on her face, her outfit was a bold statement. A short dark-blue fur-trimmed jacket hugged her figure, and she defied the chilly forty-degree temperature with a tight leopard print mini skirt.

She tottered slowly up the inclined driveway, her steps unsteady in the stiletto-heeled shiny gold ankle boots that adorned her feet, clutching a matching crocodile embossed Balenciaga hourglass handbag.

A vibrant tall young woman with sun-kissed, waist-length hair secured in a sleek high ponytail followed after, wearing simple form-fitting jeans and a stylish gray leather jacket that exuded an air of effortless cool. Chewing gum and eyes glued to her phone, the apparent bride-to-be uttered small grunts every few feet to indicate she had heard or acknowledged something said to her, but otherwise didn't respond.

Viv met them at the door. "Hi, you must be Toni and Shauna? I hope you found the place okay."

"Oh, hun, I'm so sorry!" Toni exclaimed. "We got held up at our mani-pedi appointment. Well, we were on time of course, but they claimed we didn't have an appointment. Can you believe it? I tried to tell them we had a very important place to be, but they still made us wait. But don't you know I gave them holy heck! By the time we made it to the ferry, we just missed it. Anyway, that ferry, phew! It really is something else — don't even get me started. I thought they'd at least have a cocktail bar on board to help pass the time."

While Toni spoke rapidly without taking a breath, Viv took notice of her freshly manicured and somewhat imposing scarlet nails of considerable length, in addition to the rather heavy-handed makeup and an overzealous application of Giorgio perfume.

Toni seemed vaguely familiar, and Viv had a nagging feeling that she had seen her somewhere before. Then it clicked — Toni was a dead ringer for Angie Greyson, one of the main personalities and antagonists from the reality show *Jersey Wives*! With horror, Viv recalled an infamous scene from *Jersey Wives* where a perceived slight at a formal dinner party caused Angie to throw a lamb chop at another cast member, hitting her square in the eye.

Toni handed her jacket to Viv, revealing underneath an asymmetrical hem pale-blue cashmere sweater exposing a single shoulder, plus a large ostentatious necklace of fire opal gemstones enveloped in platinum.

"Oh, this is my beautiful daughter and the bride-to-be, Shauna."

Shauna hesitantly withdrew from her phone and

demurely extended a limp hand. "Nice to meet you," she mumbled and immediately went back to scrolling on her device.

"Shauna, will you put that thing away?" her mother ordered. "We need to make sure Viv here knows everything we want for your big day. I'm just so excited!" Toni said, clapping her heavily bejeweled hands together. "Sorry, Viv, you know kids these days and their BitKlip app. I swear, she's glued to that thing twenty-four-seven!"

Shauna made a face and placed her phone in her vintage beige canvas Gucci handbag. Viv took notice of an enormous engagement ring, at least five carats, and supremely long fingernails like her mother's, lacquered bright pink, which didn't seem to prevent her from typing nimbly enough on her phone.

"Please have a seat," Viv said, showing them to the couch in her client consultation room. "Would you like some coffee or water?"

"Thanks. I could really use a latte," Toni replied.

"Oh, I'm sorry. I only have a regular coffee maker."

"That's okay, hun. We'll just stop by Starbucks on our way back to the ferry."

"Well, we don't have a Starbucks here on the island. But you can get espresso drinks at Barb's Bakery, just down the road, or at the Harborside Cafe over by the marina."

"No Starbucks! I don't know how you survive around here. This is a cute little place you've got, though. Your home office? I guess everyone needs to start somewhere."

"Thanks," Viv responded, letting the back-handed compliment slide. "What about the man I saw in the car outside? Is that your husband? Does he want to come in?"

Toni guffawed in response. "Him? Oh no, hun. That's our driver, Richie. He's fine waiting outside. That's what we pay him to do! Anyways, although lacking in some basic amenities, this island seems very charming. We first saw it on that show *Monster Brides*. The episode where the groom loses the ring on the beach and the maid of honor passes out and misses the wedding?"

"Oh yes, I'm familiar with the show."

"I don't know why Shauna can't just get married down at Saint Anthony's where we live in Newark, but she's set on having one of these trendy destination weddings, and our little girl *always* gets what she wants. I just know all my friends and followers on MyFace are gonna be real jealous when they find out where the wedding is. I can't wait to see the reaction from that old bag, Sheila! She thinks she's so much better than me, ya know the type, am I right?"

Viv, not quite sure how to reply to this, responded with a noncommittal, "Mmm hmm." She had learned in her previous profession to only open her mouth to offer an opinion when necessary.

"And I'm so glad you weren't already booked for our preferred date. I thought it'd be easier to deal with someone local for all the planning crap that needs to be done. Gawd knows I don't have time for it. My cousin Lisa offered to help pick out the dresses and everything, but quite frankly she wouldn't know a pair of Louboutins from Payless!"

"Of course Toni, I'm happy to help, that's what I'm here for," Viv congenially replied.

"Say, what kind of salons do you have here — are there any good stylists? I have the makeup part covered myself since I'm a makeup artist with my own very successful Lovely Lady Lashes business. I just made it to Double Diamond Platinum status, as a matter of fact," Toni bragged arrogantly.

There was only one so-called salon in town, Mabel's Cuttery, which Mabel ran out of her converted garage. And by observing the hairstyles of some of the town's residents who visited Mabel's shop, Viv wouldn't dare take the chance of recommending her services to any clients.

"I'm sorry to say there isn't anyone here on the island I can recommend, but I can arrange for a stylist to come for the wedding, no problem."

Toni seemed unimpressed. "Yeah, yeah, that's all well and good. Just make sure everything is social media-worthy, okay hun? I need you to ensure there are plenty of stunning photo ops. It's important that my followers on the socials see how fabulous this wedding is. And let's not forget — my little Ruffles simply must be part of the wedding party."

"Ruffles?" Viv echoed, puzzled.

"My precious fur baby! She goes nearly everywhere with me, of course. She'll steal the show in her custom-made Swarovski crystal collar and matching leash. Oh, isn't she just the cutest thing?" Toni gushed, showing Viv the lock screen photo on her phone. In it, a tiny Yorkshire terrier wore a pale lavender gown with a tiara perched on her head.

Viv struggled to keep up with the demands and eccentricities of Mrs. Giovanni, but maintained her professional demeanor.

"No problem. Ruffles is very cute and I'll be sure to include her in the wedding plans," Viv assured, sitting and pulling out her laptop. "So, how many guests do you plan on inviting?"

"We don't have an exact number yet, but it won't be too huge of an affair. We're thinking somewhere around three hundred guests?" Toni responded.

Viv hardly thought that three hundred people counted as a small affair, but kept her skillful composure. "I think that will be doable, but it is what I would consider a bit of a larger event."

"Alright, maybe so. We've got lots of extended family and friends. Leaving people out leads to hurt feelings. With our group, it's a bit of a delicate situation," Toni explained. "My husband isn't getting along very well with his uncle Gino these days either, but he's still invited, unfortunately."

"That many people should be fine, but it will limit your choice of venues here on the island. It would mean either an outdoor event or the old Masonic Hall will hold that many guests."

"Oh, so none of the cute churches will work? We really wanted our princess to have a church wedding. Our only daughter, practically an old maid at twenty-four years old, ha!"

Scoffing at this statement, Shauna glared at her mother.

"Sorry, I'm afraid none of our churches are large enough for that many guests. But the Masonic building is very nice. The ceremony room resembles a church, and you could use the ballroom for the reception," Viv explained.

"Well, that will have to do, I guess. I don't think we

want the outdoor option, too much can go wrong. What do you think, sweetie?"

Shauna, who'd been looking around bored, nodded her head vacantly. "Yeah, that's fine. But I wanted marble columns. Does this place have marble columns?"

Viv squinted her eyes, momentarily confused. "Um, no, I don't think so. Maybe we could rent some? Do you mean just a couple to frame the altar?"

"Yeah, I guess. Well, if we have to rent them, that should be okay," Shauna said, looking disappointed. "And we gotta have a chocolate fountain. You can do that, right?"

"Yes, for the reception? That won't be a problem at all," Viv replied.

"Great!" Shauna exclaimed. "Erika is gonna be so jealous. Marble columns and a chocolate fountain — I can't wait to see the look on her face when I tell her!"

"Is Erika someone you don't like whom you're not inviting?" Viv reasonably assumed.

"Actually, she's my best friend and maid of honor. Erika thought she'd be the first to marry Anthony, and she wanted these things at her wedding. But she's outta luck, it's my time to shine!" Shauna crowed triumphantly.

Choosing to ignore this revelation, Viv responded, "Okay, I'll make the reservation right away for the Masonic Hall. It requires a one thousand dollar deposit. Would you like to leave a check with me?"

"I think we'll just do a direct deposit to your account for everything just to make it easier? Then you can pay for it all as needed. Will that work?" Toni asked.

This agreement was unusual since Viv typically acted as a coordinator, arranging purchases and reservations, with the vendors invoicing the clients directly. However, she wanted to make the process as easy as possible for them. This was bound to be her biggest event yet and could lead to more business, not to mention the promise of a large commission.

"Yes, that should be fine. By the way, we haven't discussed the budget. What's the maximum amount you'd like to spend?"

"Um, I don't know. Is five hundred thousand dollars enough? We really want the best for our little girl," Toni replied.

Viv almost choked on her coffee. *Half a million dollars? Who are these people?* she thought. She could easily pull off a fantastic celebration for three hundred people for less than fifty thousand dollars.

"I would say that's more than enough. Over four hundred thousand more. I don't think you'll need to spend anywhere near that amount."

Toni rapidly fluttered her mammoth eyelashes in frustration and made a tight smile. "Okay. Like I said, we want *the* best, and we *have* the money. I'm talkin' Baccarat crystal and twenty-four karat gold-rimmed Tiffany china. Not cheap rental crap! Understand?"

Toni menacingly stabbed the table with a manicured claw, punctuating the words as she spoke. Waiting for a reply, she gave Viv a cold stare and crossed her arms.

Viv responded diplomatically, "Yes, I'm sure in that case five hundred thousand should be plenty. Well, with that settled, what about colors? Is there a particular scheme you had in mind?"

Shauna, who had since pulled her phone out of her bag and was scrolling away, looked up. "Huh? Uh, I guess I like pink and gold," she said, returning to her phone.

"Gold?" Viv asked. "You mean like orange-yellow?"

Irritated at the interruption, Shauna retorted, "I don't know, just gold."

"Okay, I think that might work best as an accent. I suggest adding something like a cream color to the mix, to go with the pink. I have some swatch books here if you want to start looking?" Viv replied.

Toni jumped up, glancing at the time. "Cream should be fine, hun. We need to get going. We'll discuss all the details later. My husband's birthday party is this evening and we need to get back. Shauna sweetie, don't let me forget to call Libby about double-checking the caterer's delivery. We don't want a repeat of last year," she said, rolling her eyes. "Gawd knows what we pay all this help for."

"Sure, whatever, Ma," Shauna replied, giving her gum an abrupt crack.

"Alright then, I'll send you the contract later," Viv said.

"Sure thing, hun. I'll have my accountant get in touch with you to wire the deposit money to your bank. And I have a list of approved vendors I want you to work with. Some old business associates of my husband's, we like to sort of help each other out. Oh, and one last thing. Do you know of a baker who can make a cake that will hide a gun?"

CHAPTER 5

This inquiry caused Viv to nearly spill her coffee on her lap. "Um, a what now? A gun!"

"Ma!" Shauna hissed. "Dramatic, much? She doesn't mean it. She's paranoid because my fiance's best man and my ex, Vince Junior, made 'threats,'" Shauna said, making air quotes. "He's just jealous, and wouldn't hurt a fly!" she exclaimed, glaring at her mom.

"Okay, maybe I am being a little overly dramatic. But you really did hurt that poor boy. I just thought we might want to have some hidden protection as an extra precaution, ya know?" Toni replied.

"I hurt him? Ha! What about Vince getting together with Erika? I don't feel sorry for him one bit," Shauna stated firmly.

"Well, sweetie, you know that Erika was also with Anthony first before you stole him away from her."

"Wow, it seems like there's a lot of complex relationship drama amongst the wedding party happening here. Do you mind filling me in?" Viv asked, perplexed.

"So first of all, I was dating Vince Junior for about a year with a lot of ups and downs. We're kinda like oil and water," Shauna explained.

"That's an understatement," Toni said with a snort.

"Anyway," Shauna continued, "During that time my best friend Erika started dating my now fiancé, Anthony, who happens to be Vince's best friend. Erika and Anthony had been seeing each other for a few months when Anthony and I started getting close. Next thing I knew, he said he thought Vince mistreated me and he was also getting tired of Erika. He said he'd break up with her if I did the same with Vince Junior."

"So that's when you started your relationship with Anthony?" Viv asked.

"Yeah, and then Vince and Erika became an item to get back at us. Vince Junior is still crazy about me and has been very angry since Anthony proposed."

"I see. Thanks for clearing that up — it's good to be aware of these kinds of issues when it comes to the preparations."

"Well, forget what I said about the gun. You'll have plenty of protection with all your father's friends there," Toni said to Shauna, smiling.

Somehow, this news didn't make Viv feel any better. Catching her breath, she said, "Okay, then. Let me walk you out."

"Sorry hun, hope I didn't scare you with that whole gun thing," Toni said with a laugh. "I swear we're not as crazy as we seem! And I know I can trust you to do a good job," she asserted, giving Viv a sharp look.

"Of course. Think nothing of it. You can count on me to make everything go as smoothly as possible."

"Okay hun, we'll be in touch. Oh! I almost forgot to give these to you."

Reaching into her handbag, Toni produced a couple of small mascara samples attached to a card.

"It's Lovely Lady Lashes," she said proudly. "I noticed that your lashes could use some enhancement, no offense. I thought you might want some like mine," Toni said, pointing at her enormous clumpy eyelashes. "This mascara has fibers that work like magic to make your lashes extra big and luxurious."

"Oh, thanks," Viv replied, taking the samples with a forced smile.

"Hun, I'm telling you, this stuff sells itself! Just put up a few posts on MyFace and you'll be raking in the cash. I make a full-time living working just a few hours a week from my phone! And if you decide you want to join my team, I'll be your personal mentor, and you'll have your own downline before you know it. Maybe even make Double Diamond Platinum status someday, like me. And you'll get a fantastic limited-edition starter kit, which has five hundred dollars worth of makeup for only ninety-nine dollars, plus the exclusive Triple L pink handbag!"

"Ma, she doesn't wanna hear about your janky mascara business," Shauna blurted impatiently, scrolling on her phone again.

"Hey, enough outta you! I just thought Viv would want to know how much Lovely Lady Lashes can change her life, that's all. Although not everyone is successful. My so-called friend, Tina, pledged to sell 300 units in one month and didn't sell a thing. Come to find out she only had 100 contacts on MyFace, so of course I dropped her like a hot potato! But I know you'll do much better than her," Toni said assuredly.

"Thanks, I'll think about it," Viv replied politely, with no intention of doing so.

"What do you know, it's my useless assistant Libby. Just a second. I gotta take this call."

While Toni was on the phone, Viv quietly remarked to Shauna, "I'm surprised your mom has this side business since it seems like she could get along just fine without it."

"Well, truthfully, she doesn't make as much money from it as she claims. I think she gets bored and this gives her something to do. And she likes the idea of being a 'boss babe' and feeling like she's contributing somehow. My dad doesn't mind because it keeps her occupied and out of his hair, even though he's paying for a lot of products that don't sell and are stacking up in the basement. Not to mention she's super annoying about it and constantly live streaming on MyFace."

Toni ended her call and rejoined them. "Okay, let's go, hun. Libby claims that everything's under control, but we'll see about that when we get home."

The sleek, black SUV sat purring in the driveway. An odd itch of curiosity nudged Viv to memorize the license plate: *K47-EGC*. As Shauna and Toni bid farewell, their chauffeur holding open the car door with a professional air, Viv returned their wave before retreating into her office.

Scribbling down the license plate number on a post-it note, she tucked it away in her desk drawer. A spark of intrigue ignited within her about these enigmatic new clients she had just met. She decided to visit Betsy at the bakery and fill her in.

The late afternoon had given way to dusk, with ominous clouds rolling in from the sea that promised rain. Embracing herself against the chill, Viv quickened her steps as a light drizzle began to patter around her. The mildly unsettled weather mirrored her current state of mind. A sudden sensation prickled at the back of her neck, causing her to whip around swiftly, only to find no one there.

BETSY WAS ALONE inside when Viv arrived, busy tidying up for closing time. "Hey, Vivi! What's up?"

"I've just had an interesting meeting with those clients from the strange phone call I mentioned previously," Viv explained.

"Ah yes, them! Didn't go quite as planned?"

"Hardly." Viv leaned closer and whispered conspiratorially, "I have this gut feeling that they might be involved with some shady business. Possibly organized crime!"

Betsy burst out laughing at this revelation. "Oh, come on, you've gotten suspicious over nothing before! Remember Mr. Jenkins from when we were kids? You were convinced he was an alien because he liked gardening at night!"

Viv laughed too but then said seriously again: "Well for starters, the mom, Toni, asked me if I knew any bakers who could hide a gun inside of a cake."

Betsy's eyes went wide. "She was joking, right?"

"Maybe. She said it was because her daughter Shauna's ex-boyfriend was making threats, but Shauna said it was nothing to worry about. And they wanted me to use their 'business associates' for the wedding vendors and insisted on a half-million-dollar budget! Plus, Toni mentioned they'd have plenty of protection from her husband's friends at the wedding!"

"Well, that all does sound a little odd, but it doesn't necessarily mean they're part of some crime syndicate! I don't think the mob even exists in this country anymore. Does it?" Betsy added, a little unsure of herself.

"I don't know about that, but I jotted down their car's license plate number. I'm hoping it might lead to the husband, since his name never came up."

Betsy rolled her eyes dramatically. "Oh Vivi, always playing detective"

Just then, Deputy Max Bennett walked in as if on cue, rubbing his hands together from the cold.

"Good evening, ladies. Wind's starting to pick up out there. Hope I'm not imposing if you're getting ready to close, Bets. Was hoping to get a coffee and maple bar for the road." Seeing Betsy's amused expression and Viv's slightly flushed face, he asked, "What did I miss?"

"My sister here thinks her new clients are in the mob!" Betsy said with a laugh.

Viv felt a heat creeping up her neck, but she held her ground. "It's just a hunch."

"Hey now, don't knock your little sis here. I know she has good instincts, so I'm sure she has a reason to be suspicious. Although I have to agree, I'm willing to guess the mafia isn't involved. So what exactly happened?"

With a resigned sigh, Viv relayed to Max the story of her meeting with the Giovannis.

Upon absorbing these details, Max looked thoughtful before saying, "Well, it won't hurt to check these folks out just to be safe. Do you have that plate number on you?"

"No, but I can get it."

"If you have time tonight, swing by the station around seven," Max suggested. "I can trace this plate for you and look up the owner."

"Okay, thanks."

The last thing Viv wanted was Max's help, but her curiosity about the Giovannis was stronger than her desire to continue avoiding him.

"Not a problem. It'll most likely be a slow night, anyway."

Betsy handed him his coffee and doughnut and chuckled. "Isn't it always after tourist season?"

"Well, I suppose so. Although last week we had those vandals over at the park playground," Max replied, reaching into his wallet to pay Betsy.

"No, don't even think of it. I was getting ready to throw that stuff out," Betsy said, refusing his money.

Max took the bills and placed them in the tip jar. "Then give it to the girls. And tell Jake he still owes me a beer from our bet."

"I'm not even going to ask. Thanks, deputy," she replied, giving a mock salute.

"Alright then, better get back to it. Viv, I'll see you at the station later?"

"Yeah, see you then."

Viv waited until Max drove away to confront her sister. "Why did you do that? I was so embarrassed!"

Feigning shock, Betsy responded, "What? I thought you needed help! Who else can help you better than an actual sheriff?"

"Deputy sheriff," Viv corrected her.

"Well, I thought you'd be grateful that I intervened.

I know you wouldn't have gone to him on your own. You do believe in fate, don't you?"

"I'm only going to see him tonight because I want to check out the Giovannis. There's nothing more to it, and never will be," Viv asserted, standing and gathering her things.

"Whatever you say, sis. Keep me in the loop, okay? Especially if I'm making a cake for them. I want to know what kind of crazy I'm really up against."

"Trust me, if that's your only involvement with these people, you're getting off easy."

"Bye! Don't stay out too late," Betsy said, winking.

CHAPTER 6

*V*iv grabbed the license plate number from her desk drawer, and at 7:00 p.m. drove over to the Manitou Island Sheriff's Department, a small and run-down brick building built in the 1970s.

Once inside she encountered Elsa Johnston, a former classmate, sitting at the main desk. Elsa was busy typing on a clackety keyboard with an ancient-looking beige computer monitor, under the harsh glare of subtly blinking fluorescent lights. The ceiling tiles were ringed with water damage and a slight mustiness wafted through the air.

"Oh my goodness, if it isn't Vivi Vogel! What brings you here this evening?"

"Hey Elsa, nice to see you. I have an appointment with Deputy Bennett. He said he'd trace a license plate number for me."

"I see. Well, Max hasn't returned yet, but I'm sure he'll be back soon. Feel free to wait here," Elsa replied, gesturing toward the row of shabby, uncomfortable-looking green vinyl upholstered seats in the waiting area. "Can I get you any coffee? I just brewed a fresh pot."

"Thanks. A cup with some cream would be great."

Elsa went to retrieve the coffee and handed it to Viv. "I heard about your mother suddenly running off with that guy — I don't know what I'd do if my mom did the same. But I'm really glad you're back in town again," she said shyly.

"Thank you, that's very sweet. Although it was an unexpected turn of events, I'm kind of glad to be back, too."

"So how's your wedding planning business going? I think it sounds like it could be a lot of fun! I just love weddings. It's exciting what's been happening on the island lately," Elsa remarked.

"I'm still just getting off the ground. Currently, I have what could best be described as some interesting new clients. Sort of the more demanding type."

"Yes, I suppose that could be a downside to the business. But you seem like just the person to handle those kinds of folks."

"Well, I'm certainly trying my best."

"I know what you mean. Working here can drive a person up the wall! Anyhow, I better get back to work. Let me know if you need anything. Max should be here shortly."

"Thank you, Elsa. I'm fine for now," Viv replied, pulling her phone out of her bag. It showed that she had a text from Toni.

Hi hun, can you please rent a storage
unit there for all the wedding stuff?
Thank u! Our accountant will be in touch
soon to get your bank info. xoxo

Viv thought it was odd that they would want to pay to store items nine months before the wedding, but figured it was their money and up to them.

Ok Toni, will do

Viv checked the time. 7:15. Elsa was talking to someone on the phone. She was deliberating if she should maybe come back tomorrow, if at all.

After her phone call ended, Elsa said, "Hey Viv, that was Max. He said sorry to keep you waiting, but he's on his way now. Should be here in about five minutes."

"Great, thanks."

Viv was almost disappointed to hear this, since she was wondering if she had made the best decision by letting Max help her. She had spent the last few months trying to erase Max from her thoughts, dodging him whenever possible.

WHILE WAITING for Max to arrive, memories of their improbable high school romance surfaced unbidden. By junior year, Viv had shed her adolescent awkwardness but remained bookish and shy. She excelled academically, leading the debate team and the French club, yet often found herself alone. Her sister Betsy, a year older and a blonde cheerleader brimming with perkiness, was her polar opposite. Their sibling rivalry was spirited but mostly good-natured.

It was Betsy who had formally introduced Viv to Max Bennett at a bonfire beach party. The salty breeze mingled with the crackling fire as Betsy coaxed Viv into staying for the impromptu post-game celebration. Max, the dashing star running back, initially struck Viv as just another superficial athlete. But under the flickering firelight, his wit and intelligence emerged. He shared her love for books, surprising her with his insights.

Their relationship blossomed for six months until Emily, Viv's friend, swooped in and stole Max away. Now, back in town, Viv has seen more of Max than she had in years, conjuring up the feelings from so long ago. The scent of ocean air and burning wood would forever remind her of that night they first met.

Soon, a car pulled into the station's parking lot, and Max walked through the door. Spotting Viv, he smiled apologetically.

"So sorry to keep you waiting, Viv. I had a call to go check out Mrs. Nelson's place. She thought she saw someone walking around the outside of her house, but it turned out to only be a deer. I hope you haven't been waiting for too long."

"No, it's fine. I've just been here for a short while," Viv replied, trying not to appear too edgy.

"Well then, why don't you come back to my office and let's see what we can find out about these people."

Viv followed Max down the short, dank-smelling corridor to his office. He pulled out his keys and unlocked the door while Viv waited.

"One sec. Just need to turn on the lights."

When finished, Max beckoned her inside. Viv looked around the cramped but cozy office and noticed how neat it looked. A pair of floor lamps and one on the desk lit the room, replacing the overhead lights. She also took note of a photo of his daughter Lizzy, but none of his ex-wife, Emily.

"Sorry about the mood lighting, but those things give me a headache," Max said sheepishly, motioning at the fluorescent ceiling lights.

"That's okay. It's actually kind of nice."

"Go ahead and have a seat," Max said, offering Viv a chair in front of his desk. He turned on a battered laptop that, from the looks of it, had seen better days.

Viv sat and pulled the license plate number out of her bag, gazing around anxiously while he waited for his computer to boot up and he logged into the system.

"Okay, let's see what we have here," Max said, taking the paper from her hand. "New Jersey K47-EGC," he murmured, typing in the plate information. "Hmm, was it a black Cadillac Escalade?"

"Yes, that sounds about right."

"Then it looks like your person of interest is a Mr. Salvatore Giovanni, from Newark, New Jersey. Birthdate January tenth, 1970. Oh, happy birthday, Mr. Giovanni. Let's see if anything comes up in the criminal database."

Max spent a few seconds clicking around and typing, then frowned. "Interesting. Says here he had a conviction for racketeering in 2001, with six weeks served and out on parole for two years. Then some additional racketeering conspiracy charges in 2012, but it doesn't say anything about prison time for those."

"Hmm... racketeering, that means fraud, right?" Viv inquired.

"Basically, yes. It's often associated with organized crime. A racket usually refers to a repeated or continuous criminal operation. My guess is this guy could be involved with some bad actors, but it's hard to say for sure without knowing the details. You'd have to do some more digging since it only shows charges and convictions in my database here."

Viv leaned back and sighed. "Well, I suppose it could be worse. At least there's nothing about murder."

"I doubt this is anything to get too worked up about. Besides, you've got me. As long as I'm around, nothing bad will happen to you."

Viv blushed, meeting Max's gaze. "Thanks. You're right, it's probably nothing. I appreciate you taking the time to check for me."

"I'm more than glad to help. I want you to know that if you need anything at all, I'm here for you. I understand that you have your reasons for avoiding me these last few months, and it's fine. But I don't want any personal stuff between us to get in the way of your safety. So please don't hesitate to call me if things get weird with these people and you need help."

Viv looked down and took a big breath. "I'm sorry about all the avoidance lately — it's pretty childish of me. I should've been more upfront with you about how I feel. The past year has been challenging, and I was afraid that seeing you again could turn into something more serious, which I'm not ready for at the moment. I just don't want to risk opening myself up to more hurt."

"I know, Vivi," Max said, quietly. "And I'm sorry if I seemed to be coming on too strong. You have to know that I care for you a lot, and I feel like I made a big mistake all those years ago. I wish I could go back and change things, but all we can do is move forward. I want what you want. And if that means just being friends, then that's fine with me."

"I'm really glad you understand. Phew! I feel so much better about things now," Viv said, smiling. She stood up and shook his hand. "Thank you for your time, Deputy Bennett."

"Anytime, ma'am," Max said, tipping his hat. "Can I walk you out?"

"Thanks, but I think I can manage."

"Okay then, don't hesitate to give me a call if you need anything."

"I won't. Thanks again," Viv replied, waving as she left his office.

Max sighed and shook his head as he watched her walk away.

CHAPTER 7

Two days later, Viv was sitting at her mother's worn kitchen table, sipping coffee and poring over the latest bridal magazines, when she received a call coming from a private phone number.

"Hello, Ms. Vivian Vogel?"

"This is she. Whom am I speaking with?"

"This is Peter Salerno, accountant for the Giovanni family. They hired you to coordinate their daughter Shauna's wedding?"

"Yes, that's correct. What can I do for you, Mr. Salerno?"

"Mrs. Giovanni has instructed me to transfer funds to your bank account to cover the wedding expenses. I'll need some information from you for the transfer."

After giving him her bank account details, he said, "Thank you very much, Ms. Vogel. And remember, you are now a trusted holder of these assets, and I assume you will do right by the Giovannis and conduct yourself accordingly."

"Yes, of course I will," Viv said, a little taken aback. "I wouldn't dream of doing otherwise."

"Just know that this is a family with lots of connections. So, we have an understanding?"

"Understood completely. You have my word."

"Excellent. The funds should reach your account within the next couple of business days. Thank you for your time, Ms. Vogel."

The line disconnected abruptly before Viv even had a chance to say goodbye. She wondered if they honestly believed that she might steal their money for the wedding. *They must be really distrustful of everyone around them,* Viv thought.

A FEW DAYS after her phone call with the accountant, Viv was in line at the First Bank of Manitou to deposit a down-payment check that she received from another client. This event was night and day compared to what she was planning for the Giovannis. Just a small, simple wedding held at the lighthouse this summer with reasonable expectations.

Viv's thoughts were interrupted when she got to the front of the line. She handed over her check and deposit slip to the bank teller, Sue. Sue had worked at the bank ever since Viv was a kid, doting on her and giving her extra candy when she came in with her mom.

"Well hello there, Vivi. Ah, I see you have another check to deposit. How's business going?"

"It's not too bad. I have a few clients lined up heading into the season. I just got a new one that's my biggest wedding yet. It will be challenging, I think, but I'm ready."

"That's exciting, good for you!" Sue replied as she brought up Viv's account. Her eyes then grew wide with disbelief. "Well! That must be quite the new client. I think we'll need to upgrade you to a personal concierge business banker from now on. Would you like to see Tom now?"

Viv stood there with a puzzled look on her face. "What do you mean? Why would I need to be upgraded?"

Sue seemed confused as well. "Oh, don't you know, dear?" She slid a printout of Viv's bank balance and recent deposits over to her.

Viv took a glimpse and gasped. Her business bank account now contained over half a million dollars in it! No wonder that the accountant had been so stern in his warning.

"What? When is this from?"

Sue, eyeing Viv quizzically, replied, "See," pointing at the transaction. "Posted yesterday. Five hundred thousand from Mancini Accounting, LLC. Was this unexpected? Maybe it was sent to the wrong account in error?"

"No, I don't think it's an error," Viv explained. "I knew that they were sending money. I just wasn't expecting to receive the entire budget up front."

"Well, that does sound a little unusual," Sue conceded. "Was this the client you were referring to with the large ceremony?"

"Yes, very large and lavish. They were discussing a five hundred thousand dollar budget and want me to take care of paying the vendors."

"Ah, well, there you go then, dear. I suppose if they have the money, they can spend whatever they want.

Though it seems a bit much for a wedding, in my opinion. Are you sure you don't want to meet with Tom? We like to give extra-special treatment to our high-value customers to make sure that your needs are being met," Sue said, smiling.

"Not right now, maybe next time. Thanks, Sue."

Viv left the bank with her head spinning. This was getting stranger and stranger. She had to call Toni.

"Hey Viv!" Toni answered. "I was just thinking about calling you today about the colors, and Shauna has some ideas about the bridesmaid dresses that we want to run by you. Oh, and you should've received the money by now."

"Yes, that's what I was calling about. I just returned from the bank. Five hundred thousand dollars?"

"Yes, hun, that's what I told Pete to send. You think it will be enough?"

"Um, I suppose so? Sorry, I thought you were exaggerating when you said that much. And I didn't think you would actually deposit the entire budget into my account all at once."

"No, I never exaggerate. Believe me, hun. There's no problem, is there? We can trust you, right?" Toni asked coldly.

"Of course can trust me! It was just a little surprising, since it's so much money."

"You bet it's a lot of money! Alright, gotta go so I can make it to my pole dancing fitness class. I'll email you about the final color palette and the bridesmaids' dresses Shauna wants to order," Toni said, resuming her cheery demeanor. A small dog yapped loudly in the background. "Ruffles, stop! You already went outside!" she snapped. "Sorry, we'll talk soon. Bye!"

Viv decided that it was time to do some extra sleuthing on just who these people were. She grabbed a glass of wine and her laptop. Viv felt a little self-conscious about drinking alone but found being by herself in the house a bit much sometimes, even in the company of Aggie.

"Okay, Mr. Salvatore Giovanni, let's see what the internet has to say about you..." Not surprisingly, there were several Salvatore Giovannis to be found online, so she narrowed her search down to Newark, New Jersey.

"Hmm... this looks interesting," she murmured to herself. It was an article from the local Newark newspaper dated July 12, 2012, with a photo of a younger-looking Toni with a man Viv gathered to be her husband, outside a courthouse.

The headline read *Local Man Ducks 2nd Racketeering Charge,* and the article outlined how Sal Giovanni had criminal charges against him dropped yet again. The latest charges alleged that his construction business was obtaining lucrative city contracts and falsely invoicing for time not worked while also inflating the cost of materials.

Viv shook her head in disbelief. The news account also practically accused Sal of paying off city officials to stay out of trouble. *Maybe my first impression about the Giovannis was right,* she thought to herself. Most of the rest of the articles she found referred to the same case, along with some various local mentions of charity events, including Sal being honored as the new president of the Columbus Day parade committee.

Suddenly, she received a new email notification — it was from Toni.

Hey Viv, heres a link to where you can buy the bridesmaids dresses, in the Electric Sunshine color. The girls sizes are listed below. Its beautiful you think? Shauna liked this one best. Will be in touch soon.

xoxo,
Toni

Viv clicked on the link to the wholesale clothing seller's website. It was a friend or "business associate" of the Giovannis, no doubt. She nearly cried out as she glimpsed one of the worst bridesmaid dresses that she had ever seen: a shapeless tea-length, bright-yellow polyester monstrosity, with a lace bodice over a cheap-looking satiny material.

The garish frock was topped off with an unnecessarily humongous lace sash that tied back into an oversized bow. It would look good on absolutely no one — which was likely an intentional choice to ensure in keeping the number one rule that no one upstaged the bride. Hesitantly, Viv ordered it in the sizes for the eight bridesmaids as instructed and emailed Toni back to let her know it was done.

As Viv took the last sip of her second glass of wine, a sense of unease settled over her. The information she had discovered about Sal Giovanni was troubling, to say the least. Maybe Max would want to know about her findings. Being a sheriff, shouldn't she keep him in the loop on what her research turned up?

She picked up her phone and, thinking twice, put it back down. She then reached for it again and found

Max's cell number. Viv's thumb hovered over the end call button, but Max answered immediately.

"Hey Viv, what a surprise! What's up?"

"Uh, hey Max. Sorry if you're busy. I was just doing some research on that guy, Salvatore Giovanni. I thought you might want to hear about it. Do you want to meet somewhere later, unless you're working?"

"No, I'm not busy. I was just finishing up my shift and will be heading home soon. I'll practically be going right past your place. What if I stop by there in about half an hour? I'd love to hear what you found out."

"I suppose that would be okay. Are you sure you have time?"

"Absolutely! I have an early day tomorrow since I agreed to do a shift trade, so it will just be a quick stop."

"Okay, that sounds fine. See you soon."

Stunned, Viv was unsure how she had just unintentionally managed to invite Max Bennett over to her place. She ran upstairs to change out of her sweats and freshen up her hair and makeup. Scanning her closet, she settled on some flattering high-waisted jeans and a cream-colored sweater.

Rummaging through her makeup, she went for a minimalist look, lining her lids with a subtle cat eye and chose a neutral eyeshadow, making her large hazel eyes pop. She decided against using the mascara sample Toni had given her. Since she was short on time, she brushed her hair back into a simple, high ponytail.

ALMOST EXACTLY A HALF HOUR LATER, she found Max knocking on her front door.

"Hey Viv, uh, nice to see you again."

"You too! Thanks for stopping by. Please, come in," Viv replied, trying to contain her nerves.

"Wow, I don't think I've been here since high school," Max said awkwardly.

"Well, honestly, it doesn't look that much different. I haven't had a chance to do much with the place just yet."

Viv had become accustomed to the 1990s decor and furniture, but was still planning on redecorating at some point. She had mostly been focused on building her business, but part of her also didn't want to let go of all her mother's things in case she changed her mind and came back home from Marrakesh. Although Barb had urged Viv to get rid of anything she or Betsy had no desire to keep.

"I think it looks great! Very homey." Max glanced around nervously, unsure of what to say next.

"Why don't you have a seat and I'll show you what I found?" Viv noted how her glass of wine might look — she hoped Max wouldn't judge her for drinking alone. "Can I get you something to drink?"

"Sure, I'll have what you're having. Not too much though," he said, gesturing toward his patrol car.

Max picked up the book on her coffee table, titled *Make it Happen: A Woman's Guide to Business and Having it All.* "This any good?"

"Um, yeah, it's not too bad," she said, slightly embarrassed. "I don't normally read a lot of self-help books, but this is all so new to me..." she trailed off. "Anyway, let me show you some of what I came across in my research."

Viv pulled up the newspaper article from 2012 about

Sal Giovanni's racketeering and fraud charges being dropped.

"Look at this. It says Sal was set to go to trial for accusations that his construction business had committed fraud. Then allegedly some kind of additional evidence came out and the District Attorney could no longer press charges. They didn't reveal publicly what the evidence was, though."

Max pointed at the article and furrowed his brow. "This is interesting. It also mentions the earlier case where he served six weeks in prison until claims of false witness testimony set him free and the racketeering charges were dropped then as well."

"I know, crazy, right? And get a load of this. It says he's known for his charitable giving, especially to the New Jersey Fraternal Order of Police, as their number one donor. They even gave him an award, and he was a guest of honor at their fundraising dinner! Sounds like a possible case of paying off the cops in plain sight, if you ask me."

"You know, Viv, I think maybe you're onto something here. This guy seems like he's up to some shady business. Now whether or not he's dangerous remains to be seen."

"Well, let's hope not for my sake," Viv remarked, downing the rest of her glass. Pouring herself another, she pointed the bottle toward Max.

"Ah, why not? Just one more. I'm still under the limit."

An hour later, they were talking and laughing about the old days. Feeling tipsy after four glasses of wine, Viv stood to grab her phone and turn up the music from its playlist. "Oh, I love this song!" The volume blasted suddenly as she stumbled over her feet, tripping over herself and landing face down on the couch.

"Whoa there, little missy. Are you okay?" Max asked, grabbing her hand to help her up.

Viv tried to laugh it off, a bit mortified. These things always seemed to happen at the worst time. Then, before she knew what she was doing, she pulled Max close and kissed him. They both paused for a moment and looked at each other awkwardly.

"Viv, are you sure about this?" Max asked quietly.

"I'm sure," she replied.

CHAPTER 8

The next morning Viv woke up to Aggie nudging her, waiting patiently to be taken outside. She sat up and winced. Her hangover wasn't so bad, but she slightly regretted what had happened the night before. Viv was a little apprehensive over her own feelings, and Max's as well. She still had no interest in pursuing a serious relationship with him and didn't want him to think otherwise. Max said he would call her later, which she was now somewhat dreading. *This could get complicated,* Viv thought.

After taking Aggie for a walk and having some coffee, Viv began feeling better and was in a great mood, in fact. She decided to stroll down to the bakery and grab some breakfast. She wasn't planning on mentioning the blossoming romance between her and Max to Betsy — she didn't need the likely interrogation following that news.

. . .

THE ALLURING AROMA of some kind of chocolate delight hit Viv as she walked in the bakery's door.

"Hey, sis. Mmm, smells great in here. Oh yum, are those chocolate muffins?" Viv asked as Betsy took a pan out of the oven.

"Uh, yes they are. You seem awfully chipper for so early in the morning. Is everything okay?" Betsy reached out to feel Viv's forehead.

"Stop, I'm fine," Viv said, batting her sister's hand away. "I'll feel better if I can have one of those muffins. Mind if I grab some juice?"

"Knock yourself out. You look hungover. Long night? Trouble sleeping again?" Betsy asked, peering closely at her sister.

Viv explained to Betsy the disturbing information she learned about Sal Giovanni.

"Wow, it sounds like you might've been right after all. Like a real-life Godfather? Better not cross these people or you might end up with an offer you can't refuse!" Betsy teased.

"Yeah, it's funny when you're not the one in a contract to do business with them. Not to mention, I have half a million dollars of their money sitting in my bank account," Viv glumly replied.

Just then, she saw Max walking in the door. *Uh-oh, here we go,* she thought.

Max noticed Viv sitting there and froze with mild surprise for a second.

"Good morning, ladies," he greeted them, stiffly, as he walked up to the counter. "Uh, looks like it's shaping up to be a nice day out there." Max cleared his throat uncomfortably.

"Hey there, Max. What can I get for ya?" Betsy asked.

"Just in for a quick bite to go. I'll have a regular coffee and… one of those muffins, please."

"Ooh, good choice! Viv likes them, don't you?" Betsy said enthusiastically, looking Viv's way.

Trying her best to remain inconspicuous in the midst of stuffing her face, Viv just smiled and gave a thumbs up, her mouth full of muffin.

After Max paid and left, giving an awkward goodbye on his way out the door, Betsy approached Viv with a smirk, crossing her arms.

"So, Vivi, you gonna tell me what's going on between you and Mr. Deputy?"

Dabbing her mouth with a napkin, Viv gazed up at her sister with the most innocent look she could muster.

"I have no idea what you're talking about."

"Ha, I knew it! Why didn't you tell me?" Betsy asked, looking slightly hurt.

"Because there's nothing to talk about. We're not in a relationship, and frankly, it's none of your business," Viv retorted.

"Okay, I get it. Jeez," Betsy muttered, holding her hands up defensively. "I just thought you'd want someone to talk to, that's all."

"I'm feeling conflicted about things right now and I'd rather not. Thanks for the concern, but I've gotta head out," Viv said, gulping down her juice. "I have a phone meeting scheduled with Toni to review some wedding details."

"Oof, good luck with that. And hey, Viv, sorry if I was invading your privacy. If you ever need me, you know I'm here for you."

"It's okay. Thanks, Sis."

As Viv returned home, she ruminated on her upcoming meeting with Toni. Her mind was filled with thoughts of Sal Giovanni and the details of the disturbing information she had learned about him. Despite this, she held onto hope that none of his alleged criminal involvement would interfere with the wedding or have a direct impact on her own life.

Entering her home, the familiar scent of lavender and vanilla greeted her, instantly calming her nerves. Viv took a deep breath and focused on preparing for the meeting ahead, determined to handle whatever may come her way.

In her office, Viv spoke on the phone with Toni, who had a TV on at full volume blaring in the background. It sounded like an argument on a reality show:

How dare you cross me like that! Do you know who you're dealing with? You better watch yourself if you know what's good for you!

"Did you look over those Tiffany china patterns and the complete list of table settings I sent, hun?" Toni squawked loudly into the phone.

"Yes, I reviewed them. Hey, can you turn down the volume on your TV? It's a little hard to hear you."

"Oh, sorry. We're watching *Jersey Wives Island: Aruba.* Ever seen it? It's fantastic!" Toni said, turning down the sound.

"Thanks, that's better. No, I don't think I've ever caught that one. So, I wanted to ask you about those quantities to make sure that they're right. Did you really mean six hundred of everything? I thought that the guest list was about three hundred people?"

"Yes, that's what I meant," Toni snapped. "We want extras in case things break. And for Shauna to keep. She won't want used dishes. And gifts for family and friends, and what-not…" Toni trailed off.

"Well, I've priced it out, and even at the wholesale rates from the suppliers' list you gave me, it will come to about five hundred dollars per set. That's around three hundred thousand dollars in total. You're spending over half your budget on dinnerware alone! You could still consider renting fine china from a place I know that offers exactly what you're buying. It will be just as elegant at a fraction of the cost…"

Toni abruptly cut Viv off. "Are you questioning *my* judgment? Because it sounds like you are. You think we can't afford this? I already told you, we want the best for our little girl, period!"

"Sorry, I didn't mean it like that," Viv insisted. "Of course you want the best for your daughter."

"Well, you better get that order in today, hun. Make sure it's delivered to the storage unit I told you to get. Oh! Also, we rented a beach house there on the island for the summer and will arrive by mid-June. We're planning on staying there off and on until the wedding. Don't think I could be away from civilization for the entire three months," Toni remarked with a snort.

"Oh, wow. You're coming here? That's great, Toni," Viv feigned enthusiastically.

"Yeah, we thought it'd be nice to get away for part of the summer and also keep an eye on things for the wedding. Not sure if my husband Sal will be able to join us much since he's so busy with everything, but I know me, Shauna, her fiancé, and some of the bridesmaids and groomsmen will be visiting. And of course, let's not forget Ruffles!" The little dog gave a sharp yap at the mention of her name.

"What about your assistant, Libby?"

"Oh, her? No hun, I fired her a few weeks ago. My third one in under two years! If you have anyone good to recommend, let me know."

"Okay, if I can think of anyone, I will. I'll look forward to seeing you all here in June," Viv tried to say with conviction.

Viv dropped the phone, slumping in her chair with a big sigh. Aggie let out a whimper and leaned against Viv's leg with concern.

Giving Aggie a hug, she said, "Brace yourself, Aggie. It's going to be a long and crazy summer!"

At that moment, Viv's phone rang, showing a call from Max. She felt slightly annoyed at him calling so soon since last night.

"Hey Viv, I'm glad you answered. I just had an interesting conversation with Al, a former police academy buddy of mine who recently transferred to the department in a town near Newark. He was reluctant to speak over the phone, but he has some info about the Giovannis we might want to know about. Wanna take a road trip with me to New Jersey tomorrow?"

MAX PICKED Viv up at 7:00 a.m. sharp the next morning to catch the ferry and meet Max's friend Al in Newark by lunchtime. Viv's pulse quickened at the thought of what she might uncover about the Giovannis on this impromptu journey. It must be pretty bad if it was too much for Al to relay over the phone.

As they made their way to the ferry, Viv noticed a book lying on the floor of Max's car. Examining it, she realized it was the same book Max had asked her about the other night: *Make it Happen: A Woman's Guide to Business and Having it All.*

Bewildered, she showed it to Max and asked, "What's this all about?"

Max flushed with embarrassment before answering, "Oh, I forgot that was there. I went down to The Book Nook and bought it yesterday. I thought it might help me understand how I can support you best."

Viv swooned a bit at hearing this. Maybe Max was serious about a possible relationship after all. But she quickly reminded herself not to get too carried away and put her guard up once again.

With a playful tone, she suggested, "Well, maybe we should start a book club." She then pivoted the conversation toward recent books they had read, trying to keep things light the rest of the way.

By 12:30, they reached their designated meeting spot: Johnny's Bar and Grill. The ancient sign was grimy and barely legible, and the building appeared nearly abandoned, with stained patches of peeling paint.

The bar was in an old, neglected neighborhood. Viv's prior visits to Newark were limited, leaving her curious about Toni and Sal's location within the city. She figured they probably resided in a more upscale area and would not run into them here.

As Viv entered the bar, her eyes adjusted to the

indoor darkness and she scanned the room. The lack of windows made for a drab atmosphere, except for a few flickering neon beer signs providing some color. Viv noted the numerous police officers scattered around, many of them enjoying lunch and some a drink or two.

"You brought me to a cop bar?" she whispered to Max with surprise.

"Don't worry, you're with me."

Viv followed Max toward a corner booth where Al was already waiting, his weathered face obscured by the dim lighting. She slid into the seat next to Max. The air was thick with the smell of stale beer and greasy food, mingling with the indistinct murmur of conversations and the clinking of glasses.

Al leaned forward, his voice barely above a whisper. "Thanks for coming, Max. And you must be Viv. Glad you could make it. I appreciate your trust in this matter." His eyes darted around the room, confirming their privacy. "The Giovannis, well, they've been causing quite a stir lately."

Viv's curiosity piqued. She wondered how much deeper the Giovannis' involvement in alleged criminal activities went, especially considering what she already knew.

Max sighed, his brow furrowed with concern. "What's going on, Al? Why all the secrecy?"

Al leaned back and took a swig from his glass, gathering his thoughts. The ice cubes clinked against the sides, a sound that seemed to echo in the heavy silence that had enveloped the table. Viv could sense the weight of Al's words before he even spoke.

"They say there's an informant, Max," Al finally declared, his voice barely audible over the backdrop of the busy bar. "Someone from within their organization has been leaking information to the police."

Viv's heart skipped a beat at the mention of a rat. Her mind raced with thoughts of danger and deceit, wondering if she had inadvertently stumbled into something far more treacherous than she had ever imagined.

"But here's the thing," Al continued, his eyes now fixed on Max. "This is not just any ordinary informant. This person knows too much. Classified details that only someone close to the Giovannis could possess. I suspect it's someone within their inner circle, someone they trust implicitly."

Max's jaw clenched as he absorbed Al's words. It meant that someone the Giovannis held dear was betraying them, putting themself in danger, and possibly risking their life.

Suddenly, brightness from the outside filled the room when another group of patrons walked in. Noise and chatter trailed off as several customers seemed to recognize no ordinary person had just entered.

Viv gave Al a quizzical look. "Who's that?"

Al glanced around nervously before responding with a whisper, "That's Gino Giovanni, head of the Giovanni organization."

CHAPTER 9

"*That's Uncle Gino?*" Viv thought to herself. He looked a lot different than she would've pictured. With his casual high-waisted slacks, frumpy sweater, battered thick-soled walking shoes, and disarming smile, he had the appearance of an ordinary friendly grandpa — not the head of a notorious crime family. Gino smiled and waved at some of the uniformed customers, who nodded at him in deference.

Al observed as Gino made his way toward a secluded table in the back corner of the restaurant. Their eyes met for a moment, and Gino's smile quickly faded into a suspicious frown. Gino abruptly dismissed Al's gaze as he sat, his two apparent bodyguards flanking the chairs next to him. Greeting them at the table were a couple of other men who didn't resemble beat cops, but detectives.

Viv and Max exchanged glances, and Al looked at his watch.

"I gotta go and make a quick phone call. Why don't

you two come meet me outside in about five minutes," Al instructed.

Viv had many questions swirling in her mind but held back from voicing them. Gino and his group were deeply engrossed in a discussion, making it unlikely that they would overhear her. Still, Viv didn't want to take any chances of others eavesdropping on their conversation. Instead, she chatted with Max about the weather, trying to fill the silence between them.

After five minutes had passed, Max said, "Alright, ready to go?"

Viv was more than ready to get out of there and curious to see what else was in store for them on this hasty visit to the Giovanni clan's home turf.

Al was waiting for them at the corner when they stepped outside. "I have to get back to work, but I've arranged for you to meet with someone who can give you more background on the Giovannis. She's available now if you want to head over there. Look for a middle-aged brunette lady wearing a red jacket."

Al handed Max a slip of paper.

"Thanks, Al," Max said gratefully. "You've been a tremendous help."

Al waved off his thanks. "It's nothing. Just be careful," he added ominously, before walking back to his car.

Max passed the note to Viv. It simply read:

Tops Diner, East Newark

"Wanna get some lunch and see what this mysterious lady in red has to say?" Max suggested as he pulled up the diner's location on his car's navigation system.

Once they arrived at their intended meeting place, Viv admired the retro-futuristic diner before them. The abundance of curved, gleaming chrome and neon made it stand out from the dreary industrial environment surrounding it. Upon entering the spacious dining room, they easily spotted their target, as the busy weekday lunch crowd had already dissipated.

A woman with short, dark hair styled into a sleek bob was seated in a secluded booth near a mirrored wall. She was carefully applying lipstick while glancing at herself in the mirror, looking up quickly as she noticed them approaching.

"You must be Viv and Max, right?" She greeted them with a warm smile, standing to shake their hands enthusiastically. Her bright red blazer had the words 'Atlantic Real Estate' embroidered on it. "I'm Lisa Rosetti-Taylor, Toni Giovanni's cousin."

Viv and Max paused in astonishment for a second at this news before taking their seats at the table. Viv thought she looked familiar before Lisa explained who she was — she strikingly resembled Toni, minus the heavy makeup.

Max was the first to speak, breaking the awkward silence and asking Lisa how she knew Al.

"Oh, we've been friends since high school. If things had turned out differently, who knows..." Lisa trailed off with an embarrassed laugh. "When Al told me about your situation, I couldn't say no. Luckily, I happened to have some free time between my house showings today."

"And what made you so willing to help us, anyway?" Viv asked directly, getting straight to the point.

"I figured you'd be curious about that. And don't worry — I won't mention this meeting to Toni or any of the Giovannis. I stand to lose a lot more than the two of you if they find out. But before I explain, why don't we place our orders first?" Lisa suggested, indicating the approaching server.

With their orders placed, Lisa took a long sip of her coffee before letting out a sigh and discretely surveying the surrounding cafe.

"I agreed to meet with you because I despise the Giovannis," she explained in a low voice. "Toni and I were practically sisters growing up; we were that close. But as soon as she met Sal after high school, everything changed. Our family comes from humble means, very conservative and religious. Our grandfather was even a police officer. So when Toni started dating Sal, who already had a well-known reputation, it was quite a shock for most of us."

Viv responded with empathy, "I can only imagine."

"Toni has always been driven," Lisa added. "She had a taste for luxury, and Sal could provide her with the best. Plus, I think she was drawn to his status and notoriety. And even now, I've never heard her question or express any remorse about the questionable origins of Sal's success and wealth."

"It's likely she's in denial. That's usually the case for those in Toni's situation," Max chimed in.

"Tell me about it!" Lisa exclaimed. "So how much do you want to know about the Giovannis?" She glanced to ensure that the area they sat in was still empty of other customers.

"As much as you can tell us," Max eagerly replied.

"Very well. So, Sal's uncle, Gino Giovanni, has been in charge of their loosely organized syndicate for the past five years, taking it over from his brother and Sal's father, Roberto Giovanni. They specialize in making loans, collecting bets, and various fraudulent schemes. Gino took the reins when Roberto disappeared after a yachting accident off the coast of Italy and was presumed drowned. Although it was widely speculated a rival gang member was responsible for his disappearance, there wasn't enough evidence, and no one came forward. So it's remained unsolved."

"Wow, so crime really is their family business!" Viv exclaimed.

Lisa nodded in agreement. "Yeah, and to complicate matters, Roberto failed to leave a will before his apparent death, resulting in a bitter family dispute over the five million dollar estate. There's especially a lot of hostility between Sal and his uncle Gino, since they each feel they should receive a larger piece of the pie than the other. Sal was made president of Giovanni Construction, receiving a hefty salary for doing virtually nothing. And although Gino built the organization with Roberto and is now in charge of the daily operations, Sal feels he is owed more, since he's Roberto's son."

"Interesting. That explains why Toni has insisted on keeping Sal and Gino at arm's length at the wedding and events," Viv mused.

"Plus, Sal was recently offended about being cut out of a deal made between Gino and New Jersey State Senator Frank Murray. Allegedly, Mr. Murray is in the pocket of the Giovanni crime family and assisted with an elaborate plot to rip off the government. They bid on a lucrative contract to build public housing at below cost, then charged the government extra for non-existent problems and unnecessary overtime. Of course, these extra charges went directly into Gino's pocket, while Sal was paid a small fraction as his cut," Lisa explained.

"What outrageous corruption!" Viv declared.

"As you can imagine, this has all created quite a large rift in the family and has split their loyalty between Gino and Sal. It's speculated that it might only be a matter of time before Sal gets his share of the estate and becomes head of the family empire by any means necessary," Lisa whispered.

"You're saying Sal might want to have his own uncle… bumped off?" Viv inquired, shocked that her initial fears about the Giovannis possibly being dangerous were proving to be correct.

"It's not easy to know what this family is capable of, but it's possible that Sal could be planning something drastic, according to rumors I've heard. And he likes to use his money to get out of trouble, as he has done before. As far as the local police are concerned, he's untouchable," Lisa replied.

"That's terrifying to think about," Max muttered, ingesting this account about the Giovanni family with some unease.

"The situation is far from ideal, and if you could keep this to yourself, I would appreciate it — especially the part about the plan involving Frank Murray. There was a small inquiry into it, but prosecutors quickly dismissed it due to lack of evidence, and Mr. Murray has since been reelected without any consequences."

"Wow, and Frank Murray is on the wedding list as a guest of honor. It's funny how accusations surrounding the Giovannis always seem to get dropped. Don't worry, we won't breathe a word of what you just told us," Viv promised.

"That would be best for everyone. I know it's a risk to tell you these things, but I couldn't stand by and let an innocent person get involved with this group without knowing what they're getting into. There's likely no immediate danger to you, but the Giovannis are unpredictable. And as you probably know, weddings can bring out the worst in people. If I were you, I'd consider quitting," Lisa cautioned.

Viv shook her head firmly. "No, I'm determined to see this through. Besides, can you imagine the backlash from Toni if I fired them as clients? She would likely do everything in her power to ruin my reputation. And since they've wired me an enormous sum of money to purchase more items than necessary for the wedding, I doubt they'll want me gone."

Lisa peered knowingly over the rim of her coffee cup and chuckled softly. "Ah yes, the money laundering. The Giovannis are constantly searching for clever ways to make their surplus cash appear clean. I'd wager that Toni's involvement with Lovely Lady Lashes is just another one of their schemes as well."

This stark realization resonated with Viv, and she gave a nod of understanding.

"And you're right, my cousin doesn't take being rejected too lightly. It is possible she could try to sabotage your business if you quit. But it's still something worth considering," Lisa emphasized.

Viv expressed her gratitude for Lisa's honesty during their meeting. "I'll make sure to remember everything you've shared," she said sincerely.

"I'm happy to assist in any way." Checking the time, Lisa added, "I have another appointment to get to now. Here's my card in case you need anything. Or if you or someone you know is looking to buy in the greater Newark area," she said with a friendly smile.

Viv wondered if Lisa was the close informant Al was referring to. She hoped not — she would hate to see Lisa put herself in harm's way by daring to speak out against her in-laws.

Viv's thoughts then drifted to Uncle Gino earlier at the cop bar, meeting with whom appeared to be detectives. Was it possible that he had turned on the family to save himself from a legal predicament? Or what about the beleaguered and now-fired assistant, Libby Greene? Surely she possessed scores of family secrets and may now choose to divulge them as revenge.

Once back in Max's vehicle, he looked at Viv with concern. "After hearing all that, you're not going to give up working with the Giovannis?"

"Max, I realize the potential risks involved, but I refuse to let fear control my choices. True, the Giovannis are a powerful and dangerous family, and there's a lot on the line. However, I'm confident in my capabilities to handle this situation. I feel I'm unlikely in any genuine danger, and the potential benefits of a substantial commission and the boost this event could give to my business are worth it."

Viv couldn't bring herself to tell Max that the main reason she didn't want to give up was because she found the Giovannis and their drama oddly intriguing, her recent yearning for excitement in her life still fresh on her mind.

"I also believe you can handle it. So… are you doing okay with everything?" Max asked cautiously.

"Yeah, I'm not exactly thrilled about working with criminals, but I doubt they'll involve me directly in any of their activities."

"Sorry, I meant about… you know, us, the other night."

With the day's chaos, they had yet to discuss the new romantic turn their relationship had taken.

"Oh, that. Of course! I just hope we can keep taking things one step at a time. We don't have to rush anything or get too serious too quickly."

"Well, you already know how I feel about you, so we can take it as slow as you want."

"Thanks, Max — for everything."

CHAPTER 10

When June rolled around three months later, Viv was busy with last-minute preparations for a beach wedding happening in two days. She had just finished a phone call with a vendor to replace a canopy that the bride disliked when Toni called to say they would arrive on the island that evening to begin their summer stay.

Viv agreed to meet with Toni and Shauna later, even though she was bogged down with tasks for her other clients. She decided that putting up with this interruption to her schedule was better than dealing with the wrath of an angry Toni.

THE NEXT MORNING, Viv found herself at the Giovannis' luxury beach house rental. Toni answered the door in open-toed pink crocodile stilettos and a hot pink zebra print kimono over a matching bikini, her skin glowing a neon orange hue. A lavish gold necklace, its chunky links adorned with dazzling diamonds, shimmered brilliantly. Her artificially plumped lips were shiny with pink-frosted gloss, and she gave Viv an air kiss on each cheek.

"Viv! How wonderful to see you. Please, come in. What do you think of the place? It's a bit rustic for my taste, but I guess it will do for a while."

Decorated in a colorful beachy theme throughout, it had four bedrooms, five baths, and a stunning ocean view. The open kitchen was starkly modern, with stainless steel appliances and a white marble countertop. The cabinets were a rich maple with glass doors, and an elegant, white tin ceiling embossed with a square pattern sat above the kitchen. An enormous window with a picturesque ocean view was the focal point of the space and overlooked an enclosed deck.

"It's nice, very charming. And you're so lucky to have this view!"

A tiny Yorkshire terrier with a pink bow perched on its head ran into the room abruptly, barking wildly at the new guest.

Shauna appeared after her, yelling, "Stop it, Ruffles! I swear that dog is gonna drive me crazy. She was supposed to be my purse dog, but for some reason she likes Ma better."

Shauna proceeded to shove the little dog out of a chair and sat down with a huff. "Wanna mimosa?" she asked Viv, raising a champagne flute and sloppily spilling some on the floor.

"No, I shouldn't, since I have a lot going on today. Thanks, though."

"Suit yourself," Shauna replied, downing the rest of her drink.

"So, Viv, did the deliveries for all the table settings

make it yet? And did you get the liquor list I sent you?" Toni asked.

"Yes, the deliveries are safe in your storage unit. And I priced out the liquor from the wholesaler you suggested. It's going to be around fifty thousand dollars for everything." Viv wondered if they would give all the surplus booze to "friends and associates," just like the tableware.

"That's all? We should've bought more!" Toni chuckled. "Hey, Shauna hun, go get your dress!"

Shauna looked up from her phone reluctantly but obediently went to fetch it.

"Oh, you won't believe how beautiful it is, Viv — belonged to our Nonna Sophia. But it needs some tailoring to fit Shauna. Is there anyone local you can recommend?"

"Sure, you can take it to Audrey Chatham's shop, A Stitch in Time over on Main Street. She does great work."

Shauna appeared with the dress, smiling. "Pretty nice, huh?"

Viv forced a smile and nodded her head. "Yes, it's lovely."

She was surprised by the sight of the gown, especially the long, ornately beaded sleeves with outdated puffy shoulders, rising at least half a foot high. Complete with a ruffled hemline, the floor-length lace and tulle dress made of multiple layers resembled a giant tiered wedding cake. Viv was confused how it could be Toni's grandmother's wedding dress, since it appeared to be a garment dating from the 1980s.

"You said this belonged to your grandmother? What year is it from?"

"Oh yes, Nonna Sophia's third wedding in 1987. I wore it myself, just three years later," Toni said proudly. "Of course, I was in a family way with our son when I married Sal, so it needs to be taken in for Shauna."

"I see. Audrey should be able to handle that, no problem." Glancing at her phone, Viv said, "Sorry, but I need to get going. Is there anything else before I leave?"

"Yes!" Toni exclaimed. "Saving the best for last. Shauna got a call back from the people at the *Monster Brides* show. She applied to be on it and they might be interested in coming here to film our little girl! My baby's gonna be famous!"

Shauna grinned broadly. "I'm so excited! I can't wait to tell all my followers. Of course, everything still needs to be confirmed."

"Oh, don't worry, they'll choose you. Didn't I always say you should be on TV?" Smiling at Viv, Toni said, "And maybe this will be your big break too, hun."

Unlikely, Viv thought to herself. She had no intention of appearing on any reality TV show, especially one like *Monster Brides.*

"Well, we'll see, I guess. So Shauna, do you mean telling your followers on MyFace?"

Laughing at this, Shauna replied, "Eww, no! MyFace is for old people, like Ma. I'm talking about BitKlip."

"Hey now, watch it," Toni replied indignantly. "Yes, that's right Viv, Shauna does her videos for her little followers."

"Little? Hardly. I'm up to just over seven hundred thousand followers on BitKlip. I think this deal with *Monster Brides* will provide some great brand synergy, as they say, and significantly boost revenue. In fact, I crunched the numbers and project to see at least a one hundred and fifty percent increase in market share in next quarter's earnings and easily make it to well over a million followers."

"Oh, that's wonderful, Shauna!" Viv replied. She was mildly surprised to learn that Shauna was such an astute businesswoman underneath her vacuous facade.

After leaving, Viv sighed and wished she had taken them up on that drink. Her head ached thinking about the potential chaos a reality show filming the wedding would cause.

Viv was walking Aggie the following week when her phone rang. Seeing it was Toni, she almost let it go to voicemail but decided to answer.

"Hey hun, are you busy?"

"Just taking Aggie for a walk. What's up?"

"You should stop by our beach house. Mark Simon is here, *right now!*"

"Mark Simon?"

"You know, Mark Simon. The famous reality show producer? Creator of *Monster Brides*? And that show *Long Island Island* where they take a bunch of unhappy couples from Long Island and make them all live together on a remote Polynesian island?"

"Oh, him. Of course."

"He thinks Shauna will be perfect for *Monster Brides*! They're gonna start filming in six weeks and he's in town to meet us and discuss production details in person. I'd like to introduce you now if you have time to come over."

"I'm meeting my sister for dinner shortly, but I could

stop by for a minute. Do you mind if Aggie comes along?"

"Of course not, hun. We're outside on the deck. See you soon!"

Upon arriving, Viv and Aggie made their way to the back of the house, which faced the shoreline. Toni and Shauna were gazing at whom Viv presumed was Mark Simon with rapt attention.

Mark, a man around the age of forty with a muscular build, donned a snug black t-shirt and a stylish leather motorcycle jacket. Despite the overcast weather, he wore mirrored aviator sunglasses. His dark, carefully coiffed hair looked like he spent way too much time and money on it, and he sported a perfectly cultivated five o'clock shadow.

As Viv drew closer, she heard him saying in a British accent, "And then I said, 'Sure, if you lose ten pounds, love!'"

"Mark, you are too funny!" Toni said with an exaggerated giggle. "Oh, look who it is. Mark, meet our wonderful wedding planner, Viv Vogel. Viv, this is the world-famous Mark Simon," Toni eagerly announced.

Mark stood and removed his sunglasses, flashing a blindingly white veneered smile at Viv, eyeballing her up and down. Reaching to shake his hand, he instead took hers in both of his, gripping it tightly, as if they were long-lost friends reunited

"My pleasure. I wouldn't say world famous, mostly just the UK and States, but I'm working on it," he said, without a hint of sarcasm.

Aggie let out a low growl toward Mark.

"Sorry, this is Aggie. She's wary of strangers

sometimes," Viv explained, as Aggie kept her eye on Mark's every move.

"Oh, no worries, love. Unfortunately, I'm terribly allergic to dogs and for some reason they don't seem to get on very well with me either."

Viv somehow managed to prise her hand away from Mark's grip and took a seat.

"Mark was just telling us about a new show he's working on called *Ghosted*. It's about people who are dating ghosts, and some are even married to them!" Toni cackled, shaking her head.

"It sounds creepy!" Shauna proclaimed.

Viv couldn't tell if she was serious or just trying to humor Mark.

"It sounds, um, interesting. So tell me, what are your plans for filming the wedding events?" Viv asked Mark, getting down to business.

"Well, we'll be there for all the big occasions as usual, plus capturing some behind-the-scenes footage in the lead-up to the big day. We'd like to film as much as possible. With the focus being on Shauna, we'll be following her around quite a bit."

Shauna smiled brightly at hearing this.

"I promise, we won't intrude too much on your plans," Mark assured.

"Since this is what Shauna wants, I won't object. As long as you don't make my job more difficult than need be," Viv curtly replied.

"Trust me, love, you'll barely even notice us."

"Let's hope so. Sorry, I'm afraid I need to run. I'm having dinner with my sister. It was nice meeting you," Viv said, giving Mark a short wave. She didn't want to make the mistake of trying to shake his hand again.

"Oh, so soon? Pity you can't stay and join us for a drink. Maybe some other time, with your husband, perhaps, or boyfriend?" Mark asked, raising an eyebrow with an amused look.

"No, neither," Viv responded matter-of-factly, irritated by his flirtations.

"Very well," Mark said, smiling. "I look forward to seeing you again in about a month, Viv Vogel." He stood and tipped his glass toward her, giving a playful wink.

At the Schooner Inn, a cozy seaside restaurant adorned with twinkling string lights and nautical decor, Viv and Betsy sat across from each other at a candlelit table. They indulged in the exquisite prime rib special and sipped on a velvety Pinot Noir as Viv recounted her meeting at Toni's luxe beach house. She revealed how the Giovanni nuptials and the events leading up to them would be televised for the world to see.

"I think it sounds exciting!" Betsy gushed. "Sis, think of how much exposure your business could get."

"Maybe. But I'm afraid that by being associated with the Giovannis in front of a national audience, I might get more clients just like them!" Viv said with a shudder. "Even though I find them strangely fascinating, I certainly wouldn't want to take on any more *Jersey Wives* clones, like Toni."

"And what about Mark Simon?" Betsy teased. "He's so good-looking! And that accent, what's not to like?"

"Well, for starters, he acts like a pompous jerk. And his shows are pure trash."

Betsy shrugged and took a sip of her wine. "Maybe you need to lower your standards a bit."

"I think what I really need is to not talk about any of this stuff for a while and finish off this bottle. Deal?" Viv said, clinking her glass to her sister's.

AS THE EVENING wore on and she returned home, Viv felt a strong need to double-check the lock at the storage unit belonging to the Giovannis. Earlier that day she had stopped by to receive the large liquor order.

Despite her certainty that she had locked the unit door before leaving, she couldn't shake off the lingering doubt. Plus, Aggie needed a walk before bedtime. The thirty-minute round trip would provide both of them with some exercise and give Viv a sense of reassurance.

AFTER SHE AND Aggie arrived at the U-Store, Viv heard some voices coming from behind the building. She thought it was a little unusual since it was almost eleven at night and wasn't expecting anyone would be around, but guessed some local person needed access to their stuff or was maybe in the process of moving.

Reaching the back of the building where the storage unit was located, Viv stopped dead in her tracks. There was a black Cadillac SUV backed up to the door of the Giovannis' unit, with two men busily moving stacks of boxes into the car.

CHAPTER 11

Under the dim yellow lights outside the unit, Viv recognized the vehicle and one of the men. It was the Giovannis' car and their driver, Richie. Aggie let out a couple of warning barks, startling the men who were focused on their work.

Richie turned and smiled as big and cordial as he could manage. This being no easy feat with his imposing build and naturally unfriendly face.

"Can I help you, miss?"

"Funny, I was going to ask you the same. Do you remember me?" Viv asked.

Richie's look went from confused to faint recognition. "Oh, you're that wedding planner gal. Viv, isn't it?"

"Yep, that's me."

"So, Viv, what brings a nice lady like you out here so late in the evening?"

"I was just coming to check the lock on the unit. I was here earlier today for a delivery. I hope it wasn't unlocked?"

Smirking, Richie dangled a set of keys from his finger. "It was locked. And don't worry, this isn't what it looks like. The Giovannis told me to come get this stuff," he said, gesturing toward stacked boxes of the liquor, crystal drinking glasses, gold-plated silverware, and Tiffany china Viv had ordered.

"Oh, and where are my manners? This is Tommy, Sal Giovanni's cousin and business partner," Richie said, jerking his thumb toward a man even larger than Richie, who had been silent so far.

"Good to meet you," Tommy said, stepping forward and extending his huge mitt for Viv to shake, giving her hand a tight squeeze. "Nice dog you got there." He pointed his cigar at Aggie, who gave another cautionary bark.

"Thanks. Toni didn't mention that someone was coming to pick up anything."

"Well, if you don't believe me, I'd be happy to call her," Richie replied, reaching for his old-fashioned flip phone, which was secured in a holder clipped to his belt.

As he lifted the phone, a glint of silver flashed from the grip of a pistol tucked into his waistband.

"No, it's okay," Viv insisted.

She reasoned that even if the Giovannis did not approve this pickup of goods, what could she do anyway? The pistol's presence made it clear that these were people who didn't appreciate a hassle.

"No need for concern. We're leaving plenty for the wedding. Enough for everyone to have a great time. You know the Giovannis never spare any expense with these things."

"Yes, they've made that very apparent. I guess I should get going. Don't forget to lock up."

"You know, it's getting late for you to be out walking alone. Why don't you let us give you a ride? It wouldn't be too much trouble. I already know where you live."

"Um… thanks. But it's such a pleasant night and Aggie needs the exercise and all — so uh… I think I'll just walk."

"Okay then. Be safe out there, Viv Vogel. Ciao!" Richie replied.

IT TOOK MORE than half a block before Viv's pounding heartbeat returned to normal. Recalling her conversation with Lisa, she now seemed certain that her clients were using her to purchase items they were then taking and likely planning on reselling or trading to launder their ill-gotten gains.

Even though it was late she texted Toni, who confirmed that she had asked the men to come to pick up some of the goods from the storage unit and bring them back to Newark.

Viv thought it might be a good idea to call Max and update him on the latest developments with the Giovannis. Max had just finished his shift and said he would stop by to see her.

MAX ARRIVED about twenty minutes later. "So, what's this all about? Are you okay?"

"Yes, I'm fine. Just a little shaken up since it does seem true that the Giovannis have involved me in some type of money laundering scheme." Viv went on to explain what happened at the U-Store.

"I should see if I can find them to check things out," Max replied when she finished.

"Max, please don't. Toni instructed them to pick up the items, and I don't want them thinking I called the police on them. Besides, the last ferry for the night just left a few minutes ago. I'm sure they're on their way back to Newark by now."

"You have a point there, but I'm going to have a look around just in case. And I'll make some phone calls tomorrow to see what else we can find out about the Giovannis."

"You should be careful about whom you talk to and asking too many questions. They've probably paid off half of the law enforcement in New Jersey. Someone might tip them off."

"Don't worry. You know I won't let anything happen to you."

"It's not me that I'm worried about," Viv said, grabbing Max's hand.

THE FOLLOWING MORNING, they went to have breakfast at the Schooner Inn. Viv didn't mind returning there for a second day, as it offered some of the best food on the island. The aroma of freshly brewed coffee and sizzling bacon greeted them as they entered. Viv's spirits had lifted, and she pushed the previous night's incident to the back of her mind.

She was scanning the menu, trying to decide between the eggs Benedict or pancakes, when Viv heard a British-accented man snap his fingers and demand loudly, "How about some service over here, love?"

Please don't let it be him, she thought. Viv turned

around and sure enough, it was none other than Mark Simon sitting at the table behind theirs.

"Ah, good morning, Viv. And Deputy," Mark said, flashing a raised eyebrow and knowing smile at Max.

Viv and Max shared a bewildered look. Max was off duty and in civilian clothes, so Viv was wondering how they knew each other and Max was likewise curious how Mark knew Viv.

"Fancy running into you two at such an early hour. I didn't know you were, ahem, friends," Mark commented, smiling mischievously.

Max pretended not to hear him and continued perusing the menu.

"Hello, Mark. Yes, Max and I are friends. What about it?" Viv responded brusquely.

Ignoring Viv's reply, Mark said, "Lovely morning, isn't it? Deputy Max, I promise to behave this time," Mark insisted, placing his hand over his heart. "You'll hardly even notice our presence."

"For your sake, I hope so, Mark," Max cautioned. "You know your permit to film on the island depends on it. We won't tolerate what happened the last time you were here."

"I one hundred percent take the blame for that unfortunate incident. You have my solemn word it won't happen again. I guarantee we'll cause you zero problems. Well, I'll leave you alone to enjoy your breakfast. I look forward to seeing you both when I return with my crew in August."

"Okay, whatever you say, Mark," Max replied.

Viv was curious about Mark's revelation, dying to know what "unfortunate incident" he was referring to. She was grateful when their food finally arrived, but struggled to maintain a conversation, knowing that Mark was surely eavesdropping on every word. Despite only meeting him yesterday, she already harbored a deep aversion toward him.

After finishing their breakfast, Max asked the server for the check. With a bright smile, she replied, "Actually, Mr. Simon here has already offered to pay for your meals."

Mark bowed his head with faux embarrassment and hoisted his Bloody Mary. "Cheers. It was the least I could do."

Joining Mark at his table, Max responded, "Thanks for the gesture, Mark, but I can't accept it."

"Oh, is breakfast considered bribery? I was only trying to be nice."

"One could perceive it as an attempt to influence a public official, so yes, technically, it is bribery. Thanks again for offering; it's not necessary. Judy, I'll take the check, please."

"I guess you know best. Enjoy your day, you two," Mark replied dismissively.

ONCE OUTSIDE, Viv and Max burst out laughing.

"I didn't know you had the pleasure of already being introduced to Mr. Simon," Max said.

"Yes, just yesterday, unfortunately. The Giovannis had him over at their beach house and wanted me to meet him because he could disrupt the entire affair. So, I have to know what happened the last time they were here filming?"

"Ugh," Max said, making a face. "He caused a huge ruckus at the Old Lighthouse Inn. Mark was hosting a late-night party and a bunch of guests complained to the staff. They tried to kick him out, and he got irate, refusing to leave and claiming he was famous and could do whatever he wanted. I ended up arresting him and gave him three days to finish filming and to leave town by."

"Wow, why am I not surprised?"

"So, you're not charmed by Mr. Reality?" Max asked playfully.

"If you think I would find that guy charming, then you don't know me very well."

"I knew there was a reason I like you so much, Viv Vogel," he teased.

"I hope you'll remember that, Max Bennett."

LATER THAT EVENING AT HOME, Viv's phone pinged with a new email from Laura Mitchell, an old acquaintance and reporter for the local newspaper, the *Manitou Gazette*. The subject line simply stated, "Coffee?" In the email, Laura mentioned receiving information from a colleague about some of Viv's clients and suggested they meet up for coffee and a walk to discuss it.

Viv assumed that this had to do with the Giovannis, her only noteworthy clients at the moment. Living in a small town, news traveled quickly, so it seemed a given that Laura knew she was coordinating their wedding.

Her curiosity piqued, Viv responded to Laura, suggesting that they meet up the following day at the Harborside Cafe. She anxiously wondered what kind of information her old acquaintance had stumbled upon. Thinking about potentially uncovering more dirt on the

Giovannis made her giddy with a mix of fear and excitement.

THE NEXT MORNING, Viv arrived at the cafe earlier than planned. The Harborside Cafe exuded a homey maritime charm that embraced Viv as she stepped inside. Vintage nautical maps, faded pictures of old sailing ships, and brass portholes adorned the walls. Dimly lit lanterns hung from the wooden beams overhead, casting a warm glow over the space. The air was redolent with the inviting scent of freshly baked buttery pastries.

Viv found a secluded corner table near a large picture window offering a panoramic view of the bustling harbor outside. She settled into the worn leather chair, her eyes drifting over the eclectic mix of patrons scattered throughout the cafe.

Fishermen with weathered faces sat huddled over steaming cups of coffee, their rough hands wrapped around the ceramic mugs. A crowd of tourists, all dressed in fancy attire seemingly for a wedding, snapped photos and let out carefree laughter. And some artists in paint-splattered smocks sipped espresso, chatting animatedly at a nearby table.

As Viv languidly stirred her coffee, her mind wandered to all the secrets and dangers surrounding the Giovannis. The weight of their presence in her life was becoming increasingly burdensome. While Viv was lost in thought, Laura Mitchell bounded through the cafe door, her vibrant red hair catching everyone's attention. She spotted Viv and made her way over, a determined expression on her face.

"Viv! It's been too long," Laura exclaimed, taking the seat across from her. "How have you been?"

"Busy, but good," Viv replied with a smile. "Why don't you grab a coffee and we take a walk? I can't wait to hear what you've found out."

As THEY ENJOYED their coffees and strolled along the picturesque streets lined with colorful summer blooms, catching up on their lives, Viv finally had to ask what this meeting was all about.

"So, Laura, what exactly did your colleague tell you about my clients?" she asked, unable to mask her anticipation.

Laura lowered her voice and scanned their surroundings cautiously. "My reporter friend dug up some interesting details about the Giovanni family and their crew. She works for a well-known newspaper in the city and her specialty is investigating organized crime. I thought someone should inform you about these affairs since I wasn't sure how much you already know. I only ask that you keep this information close and not reveal the source."

"You can trust me Laura, promise. I've already pieced together some of their secrets. What did you find out?"

"She discovered that Anthony, the groom, and his best man, Vince Junior, are under investigation. They both work for Sal Giovanni at Giovanni Construction, another part of their criminal empire. According to reports, law enforcement recorded Vince Junior attempting to make a covert agreement with Senator Frank Murray. The deal involved him working with Sal to secure some fraudulent public projects and steal from the government."

"Well, well... it seems like we have more shady characters in our midst," Viv remarked.

"Yes, and Senator Murray was previously accused of a similar arrangement with Gino Giovanni, but the evidence was lacking. Now, he is wary of working with Sal because of the investigation and doesn't want to betray his previous ties with Gino. Despite this, Vince continues to pressure Mr. Murray into reconsidering."

"And I recall Toni having reservations about Vince Junior and not speaking very highly of him."

"Nonetheless, Vince is doing whatever it takes to climb the ranks in their organization. He thought that by dating Shauna it would be an easy way in, but then she left him for Anthony. It must have been an immense blow for Vince," Laura commented.

"I know all too well about the drama between Shauna and her ex. These certainly aren't my typical clients, but I'm resolved to finish the job I was hired for. Thanks for bringing this to my attention. I just hope that no one gets arrested before the wedding. I have no idea how to prepare for a jailhouse ceremony."

Upon returning from her meeting with Laura, Viv sought out Max to discuss the new information she discovered.

Max listened intently as Viv relayed the details. He was both concerned and intrigued at hearing these additional facts. It seemed like each day brought them closer to the heart of the Giovannis' web of secrets.

"This Vince Junior sounds like a loose cannon," Max remarked, his voice filled with caution.

Viv nodded in agreement. "I know, Max. This just adds another layer to an already volatile situation."

Max reached out and squeezed Viv's hand reassuringly. "We're in this together. I won't let anything happen to you or your plans for the wedding."

A sense of determination washed over Viv as she looked into Max's eyes and felt his unwavering support. She knew they were in this together, facing whatever challenges lay ahead.

CHAPTER 12

By the time the calendar turned to August, Viv felt the increased tension of the impending Giovanni nuptials. The wedding was only a month away, and Toni's constant micro-management was wearing her nerves thin. To top things off, the *Monster Brides* crew was set to arrive in town today, along with the rest of the wedding party coming throughout the week.

Viv tried to put all this out of her mind by diving into a cleaning frenzy. She was engaged in clearing out and wiping down the kitchen cabinets when her phone rang. It was Betsy. This was unusual since normally they just texted.

"Hey Bets, what's up?"

"Hey Viv, I don't know what you're doing right now, but you should get down to A Stitch in Time as soon as you can. I saw the *Monster Brides* film crew and heard a bunch of commotion, so I peeked through the window. You might want to see what's going on with your clients. Audrey doesn't look too happy."

The bakery was just a couple of doors down from

Audrey's seamstress shop, where Shauna was trying on her altered wedding gown today. Viv didn't realize the film crew intended to document the fitting.

"Oh, crud. Thanks Bets, I'm glad you called. I'll head over there right away."

Viv arrived at Audrey's shop and managed to squeeze her way through the door. The small store was brightly lit and crammed with a lighting rig, two cameramen, someone holding a giant boom mike, and a gangly red-haired young guy with an earpiece and clipboard, giving Viv a vicious glare as she attempted to walk in. Toni, Shauna, and of course, Mark, were there as well.

"This is a closed set!" the guy with the clipboard hissed.

"It's okay, I'm the wedding planner," Viv replied assuredly, pushing past.

In the middle of the room, Shauna was busy yelling a tirade of insults at Audrey. Mark stood off to the side, arms crossed, with a satisfied grin on his face.

"Oh Viv, thank goodness you're here. Will you please tell her this isn't my fault?" Audrey pleaded, pointing at Shauna.

To say that the freshly altered gown was ill-fitting would be an understatement. It was so tight it was a wonder that the zipper had managed to hold itself together, and appeared as if she would need something heavy-duty to be released from its clutches.

Although hesitant to be on camera, Viv stepped in between them.

"Tell her she's ruined my dress and my wedding!" Shauna wailed.

"Okay, calm down. Let's try to work this out. Audrey, you're sure you got the correct measurements?" Viv asked.

"Viv dear, I've been doing this for over thirty years, and I'm one hundred percent positive that I measured her and took in the dress correctly. This happens all the time! She gained a little weight after the first fitting. It's not…"

Enraged, Shauna cut Audrey off. "Whoa. Wait! Are you calling me fat?"

"That's not what she's saying at all. Audrey, please continue," Viv replied.

"What I've been trying to tell them for the last fifteen minutes is that I've left plenty of room in the seams to let the dress out some more. I can have it finished by tomorrow."

"Shauna, is that acceptable to you?" Viv asked.

"Yeah, I guess so," Shauna responded reluctantly.

"Okay then. Glad we have that sorted out," Viv replied.

"Cut! Cut!" Mark yelled with annoyance. "Shauna, love, let's do this again. Don't listen to Viv. I want you to show some genuine emotion this time. This woman has just ruined your wedding dress! Now, I'd like to see something more extreme. I know, why don't you knock down that mannequin over there while you're shouting? Remember, you're very angry!"

"Hey, wait a second!" Viv exclaimed. "Audrey doesn't deserve this."

"Audrey doesn't even need to be in the scene. We've got plenty of footage to edit in post-production," Mark replied.

"I'm not going to stand by while you disrespect

Audrey and her shop," Viv retorted, hand on her hip. "Audrey, do you want these people to stay and continue filming?"

Shaking her head no, Audrey replied, "I'm sorry, but I'd like you all to please leave."

Frustrated that his production was just stopped, Mark shot Viv a withering look. "Alright everyone, you heard the lady. Let's wrap it up. We'll just get some green screen footage with Shauna and fix this in post. You'd be amazed at what our talented production team is capable of, Viv."

"Are you going to allow them to use this footage in the show?" Viv asked Audrey.

"I already gave them permission," Audrey said regretfully.

"That's right," Mark confirmed with a smirk. "Ethan has her signature on the waiver." He pointed to the pale ginger-haired man with the clipboard. "Ethan, come here for a second. Viv still needs to sign a waiver."

Ethan suddenly appeared and shoved some papers toward her, causing Viv to seethe with outrage. "I'll never agree to appear on one of your stupid shows! Edit me out in post," she replied, throwing the papers at Mark as she turned to leave.

"Suit yourself. You've got no camera presence, anyway. Viv Vogel, the hero. Ha! She should stick to wedding planning if she knows what's good for her," Mark said in a low mutter.

Like a bird of prey, Toni swiftly clutched Viv by the wrist on her way out the door, digging in with freshly manicured claws.

"Hey, I know this lady is your friend and all, but I'd appreciate it if from now on you didn't interfere with the show. This is my baby's dream and I won't let anyone ruin it!" Toni threatened.

"Toni, I'm sorry, but I wasn't trying to ruin anything. Audrey said she'd fix the dress. She doesn't need to be a part of this. She's a good person. That's the only reason she agreed to let the crew in and signed the waiver. And I realize you like him, but personally, I think Mark Simon is kind of a jerk," Viv said loudly, making sure that he heard.

"Fine, whatever," Toni replied, releasing Viv from her talon-like grip. "I'll call you tomorrow about the flowers."

Viv left Audrey's shop and headed to the bakery, her face flushed with anger.

"Uh-oh, what happened?" Betsy asked.

"Betsy, whatever you do, do not allow that crew to film in here or sign the release to appear on their show." Viv recounted the tense scene at A Stitch in Time.

"Wow, that is so crazy!" Betsy exclaimed. "I can't believe Mark Simon is directly telling everyone what to do and altering the footage."

"I know, so much for the 'reality' in reality television, right?"

Glancing out the bakery's window, Viv was appalled at what she saw. Mark Simon and his production assistant, Ethan, had stopped outside the bakery and proceeded to waltz in. Ignoring Viv, Mark paused at the front counter and peered at the menu.

Betsy's mouth dropped when she noticed who it was. Giving Viv a nudge in the ribs with a sharp elbow, she quickly hopped behind the counter, staring at the celebrity television producer who had just wandered into her shop.

"Hi there, love. One coffee to go, black."

"Coming right up. Are you sure you don't want anything else? Croissant, doughnut? I'm closing soon so it's on the house. You're Mark Simon, right? If you don't mind me asking."

"Ah, thanks, love, but no thanks. Gotta keep fit," Mark replied, running his hand over his tight-shirted midsection. "And yes, I am he," he said, grinning broadly at the recognition.

"Well, it's nice to have you here in town. My sister can't seem to stop talking about you."

Viv gave Betsy a scowl, making a mental note for retribution later.

"Your sister, aye? Have I met her?"

"Oh, I think you have. Hey Viv!" Betsy called out, even though she was sitting just a few feet away. "Mark Simon is here!"

"Hey Mark," Viv said flatly.

Mark snapped his fingers sharply at Ethan, indicating for him to pay. Ethan, who'd been sitting and scrolling through his phone, jolted to attention.

"Get over there and pay the lady, you ginger sloth! Hard to find good help these days," Mark muttered irately, as he took a seat across from Viv with a sheepish look.

"Viv, I'm so glad I ran into you. I'd like to apologize. Sometimes I get a bit, well, passionate on set. And after rewatching the scene, frankly, I think it's just brilliant. I didn't mean what I said about you not having a camera presence. I admit I was rather upset about you bringing down Shauna's tantrum, but I think you brought in a nice change of pace. Like a strict mom kind of vibe, you know? Or, uh, maybe like a wild animal trainer. We'd really like to see you interact with Shauna more on camera. Will you reconsider signing the release form, please?"

"Thanks for the apology, but there's no way I'll agree to be on your show. And you should be apologizing to Audrey, not me."

"Well love, I think you're making a big mistake and wasting an opportunity to promote your business to millions of viewers, but it's your choice. Here's my number if you change your mind, or would like to get together to discuss this further," Mark said with a wink, handing Viv his business card.

Viv reluctantly accepted the card. "Thanks, but don't hold your breath."

"Alright then. Ladies, see you soon, I hope," Mark called out as he and Ethan left.

"Not if I can help it," Viv muttered.

Betsy snatched the card away from Viv. It read:

> Mark Simon
> Creative Visionary
> Simon Says Entertainment

"Sis, are you crazy? I know he seems like a jerk, but he's right. You're passing up a huge business opportunity here. Plus, you're single! Did you see the way he was looking at you? I know I'm married, but wow, all I could think about was how ripped his abs were."

"Bets, are you out of your mind? You think that I'd be even remotely interested in him or his ridiculous show? Creative visionary? Oh please. More like delusional dullard."

Viv grabbed the card back from Betsy and started to crumple it, but then paused and smoothed it out. She thought, *who knows when this might come in handy*, throwing it in her bag.

CHAPTER 13

*L*ater that week, Viv was busy working with the florist on the arrangements, ordering the cake from a bakery in Providence, and making final plans with the Bon Jovi cover band Shauna and Anthony requested for the reception. A frantic call from Toni interrupted her work.

"Viv, you gotta get over here to our place, quick! Oh my gawd, someone's ruined our beautiful heirloom dress! Please, drop whatever you're doing and hurry!"

As Shauna's deafening shrieks echoed in the background, Viv knew that this was the last thing she needed to deal with.

Taking a deep breath, she responded, "That's horrible! Of course, I'll be there in just a few minutes."

Viv arrived at the Giovannis right away, just as Mark and his crew were packing up their equipment and leaving.

"Bloody awful situation in there," Mark declared

when he spotted Viv. "Shauna told us to stop filming. She's gone mad! Can't really blame her, though," he said, shaking his head.

Ignoring his presence, Viv marched up to the door where Shauna stood holding the ruined wedding gown and sniffling.

"Can you believe this?" Shauna exclaimed in a high-pitched voice.

The wedding dress was cut in long strips from the top of the bodice all the way down. There was no way it could be salvaged.

"Oh, Shauna, I'm so sorry. This is terrible!" Viv exclaimed as Shauna burst into fresh tears. "I know this dress is special and the one you wanted to wear, but I have some connections at a couple of boutiques in New York. They could get you fixed up with something new in plenty of time for the wedding."

"I guess I have no choice, but it won't be the same! I'm gonna murder Erika, I swear!" Shauna yelled, stomping her feet.

Toni patted her arm reassuringly. "Now hun, no one saw Erika do it and all the girls were here last night."

"Who else but her would've done it, huh? She's jealous of me!" Shauna snapped at her mother.

"Hun, they're all jealous of you. Why don't you sit down and I'll bring you a glass of Chardonnay," Toni replied soothingly. "Viv, will you come help me out in the kitchen?"

Viv followed Toni across the vast room into the kitchen, where Toni began pulling bottles from the wine rack, looking at the labels.

"I didn't want to make Shauna more upset, but I'm leaning toward Erika too," Toni said in a low voice.

"Do you seriously think the maid of honor would do something like that? Aren't they best friends?"

"Well hun, I would say 'friends' loosely. They've been competing with each other since middle school. And it's worse now that Shauna's marrying Erika's ex-boyfriend. It's not Shauna's fault that Anthony liked her better!" Toni exclaimed, tightly gripping the bottle of wine she selected.

"Were there many people over last night who might have had access to the dress?"

"Yes, we had a little party with all the bridesmaids and groomsmen, plus their partners."

"So Vince Junior was here with Erika? I thought Vince was making threats."

"Vince Junior? Yeah, but he's okay. He and Anthony have a truce worked out for now. Besides, I just don't see Vince doing this. It seems more like something a woman would do, ya know?"

"Hmm… maybe so. When was the last time Shauna saw the dress intact?"

"Well, we got it back from Audrey yesterday afternoon and she tried it on and showed it to the girls last night, then put it back in a zipped-up bag in her closet. She looked fantastic in it after the alteration! The girls were all just raving. I'm so upset that our beautiful gown is ruined," Toni sobbed, dabbing away a tear.

"Anyone could have gone into her room during the party after she tried it on. Were there any arguments? And what about today — who else has been here besides Mark Simon and his crew?"

"Oh hun, everyone was drinking at the party. Shauna and Erika bicker all the time and were doing the same last night. I'd say everything seemed normal. And it was only Mark Simon and the crew here today to film Shauna trying on her altered dress."

"Why didn't they come to film during the party? Would they have had any access to the dress today?"

"It was sort of a last-minute gathering and the crew being here today was already planned to give enough time for Shauna to get the dress back. Mark wanted to have more of a special moment with her showing me the dress and explaining how much it meant to her. There's a reason she got so upset at Audrey's," Toni murmured, wiping away mascara-streaked tears.

She then abruptly snapped her head toward Viv and scowled. "Wait, you're not trying to blame this on Mark, are you?"

"Toni, I'm not blaming anybody. I just wanted to see who could have had access, that's all. At this point, I feel like it could be anyone."

"Anyone? Ha. Don't you forget, it's Mark Simon who's gonna make my baby a star. No one's getting in the way of that!" Toni hissed, poking a hot-pink lacquered claw toward Viv. "So, why don't you text me the names of those dress boutiques when you get a chance, okay? Wine?" she asked with a forced smile, handing Viv a glass.

The doorbell rang, and Ruffles began barking furiously. "Ruffles! Get out of the way!" Shauna yelled, storming to the front door. "Oh, Vince Junior, what do you want?" she asked, exasperated.

"Hey Shauna, can I talk to you for a sec?"

"Yeah, I guess. Come in."

Glasses of Chardonnay in hand, Toni greeted Vince in the living room. "Why hello again, Junior. Back so soon? What can we do for you?" Toni flashed him the same frozen grin she had given Viv a moment before.

"Well, I uh…" Vince trailed off. Seeing Viv standing near Toni, he paused and nervously ran his hand through his perfectly styled mullet.

"Look, Shauna. Erika's real upset about you accusing her of messing up your dress and stuff. You need to lay off. Somehow, I get the feeling you're jealous of me and her being together. When you broke up with me, you stole her boyfriend, remember? The one you're now engaged to? Haven't you treated your so-called best friend bad enough?"

"Exactly! She's the one who's jealous, not me. She always talked about getting married to Anthony, even though they were only together for five months. He thought she was crazy and wanted to get away from her! That's not my fault," Shauna retorted.

"Crazy? You're the crazy one here, Shauna. And I'm telling you, if I hear any more crying from Erika about you accusing her of sabotaging your wedding, you'll be sorry!"

Turning abruptly, Vince walked out the door and slammed it behind him.

Shauna flung open the door and yelled, "You're going to get it now, Vince Junior! You won't just be sorry… you, you'll be the one sorry!" Shauna stammered angrily, as Vince jumped into his vintage Camaro and peeled out of the driveway with a squeal.

"The nerve of him coming here like that. Can you believe it?" Toni asked incredulously.

· · ·

THAT EVENING, Viv was at home putting the stressful day behind her by relaxing in her comfy flannel pajamas on the faded floral print couch, when she heard a loud thud come from the front of the house. A car drove away with screeching tires, causing Aggie to wake with a startled bark.

Viv ran outside to see the taillights of an unidentifiable car speeding into the distance. She noticed a big gouge in the wood siding under the window of her enclosed porch. Nearby was a brick, with a scrap of paper rubber-banded around it.

Viv picked up the brick and examined the piece of paper. Scrawled in all capital letters, it said:

STOP THIS WEDDING OR ELSE!!!

CHAPTER 14

Viv naturally assumed that the note meant the Giovannis' wedding. Reluctantly, she realized that she should call Max and have him come out to investigate. She was reluctant because she had been keeping him at arm's length the last few weeks since she was still having reservations about getting involved in a serious relationship with him. But she knew calling the police was the right thing to do.

After Viv explained what happened, Max said he would come over immediately. She decided to look around the perimeter of the house with Aggie to check for anything amiss.

Max arrived quickly and gave Viv a big hug, asking if she was okay.

"I'm fine, really. I'm pretty sure this is nothing. Earlier today Toni called and asked me to come over since someone cut up Shauna's wedding dress. They think it could be the maid of honor, Erika. Then Vince Junior made an appearance and threatened Shauna for blaming Erika."

"Hmm, that happened today also? Did you see anything tonight, like a car or anyone suspicious?"

"No, the car had already sped off by the time I came outside. I'm just glad they were a lousy shot and missed my window."

Max walked around the yard with a flashlight, checking every inch of it for additional clues. Not finding anything of further interest, he picked up the brick and the note, securing them in his satchel.

"Stay safe and keep your doors and windows locked. I'll drive by later to check on things."

"You don't have to do that. I'll be fine."

"Viv, not only is it my job, but I want to. I'll be in touch if any leads turn up."

ONCE INSIDE, Viv called Toni to let her know what had happened.

"Hey Viv! I'm so glad you called. We have a few changes to make with the seating arrangements at the reception."

"Hi Toni, something weird just happened." Viv described the attempted window vandalization and the brick with the note.

"Oh, they did the same thing to us tonight! Busted right through Shauna's car window. She was so mad!" Toni exclaimed.

"Did you call the police?"

"Police? For this? No hun, we take care of our problems ourselves. Shauna was in a real tizzy right before Mark and his crew arrived for some more filming tonight. She wanted to go find Erika and straighten her out, and the cameras will be there too when she does!

Ah, I better let Shauna know that the same thing just happened to you. We'll talk soon, hun. Bye!"

TEN MINUTES LATER, Max received a radio call from dispatch about a disturbance at the Waves Rolling Inn. When he arrived, he found a huge spectacle of cameras, lights, crew, and at least three people shouting over each other. Mark Simon stood off to the side, looking very pleased with the heated commotion he was documenting. Spotting Max's arrival at the scene, Mark sighed with irritation and acknowledged him with a tense nod.

A tall woman with long, dark blonde highlighted hair, whom Max assumed to be Shauna Giovanni, was excitedly waving a piece of paper similar to the one found at Viv's.

"How do you explain this, then!" she screamed at a stunned petite young woman with curly brown hair, clad in a t-shirt and pajama shorts. "And my ma just texted me that you did the same thing to our wedding planner? How could you!"

Max guessed that the woman facing Shauna's tirade was Erika, per Viv's description of the situation.

"Shauna, I'm telling you, I didn't do this! I've been here with Vince all night, haven't I babe?" Erika whined, turning to a lanky, bare-chested man sporting a blond mullet, clad only in boxer briefs.

Max knew this must be the infamous Vince Junior, who proceeded to shout over Shauna's accusations.

"Alright people, let's settle down here. Someone want to tell me what's going on?" Max bellowed with authority as he reached the door of Room 15.

"Officer, she broke my car window with a brick, and did the same at my wedding planner's house, and this note was on the bricks!" Shauna exclaimed, holding up the note. "Because she's jealous!"

"Did you see her do this either time?"

"No, but who else would want to see my wedding called off? And she ruined my wedding dress!"

"Did you see her ruin your dress?"

"Well, no, but I just know it was her!"

"Okay, here's what's going to happen. I need you both to leave," Max said, pointing at Shauna and Mark.

"But I…" Shauna started.

"Zip it. And I need you two to get dressed and come with me," Max commanded to Erika and Vince Junior. "We're gonna get this straightened out. You're not under arrest. I just need to ask you some questions."

"Ha, jailbirds! Right where they belong," Shauna taunted with glee.

"One more word out of you and you're coming along too," Max warned. "And gimme that piece of paper. It's evidence."

Shauna handed him the note with a grin, waving to Erika and Vince as they went inside to get ready to go to the police station.

"Just can't seem to stay out of trouble around here, huh, Mark?" Max asked with exasperation, turning his attention to Mark Simon.

"Look, Deputy Bennett, we simply followed Shauna to this location to film for the show. We had no idea what she was planning and weren't trying to start any trouble, I promise," Mark insisted.

"You know I mean it when I say I have no problem making sure your film permit gets pulled immediately.

Any more incidents or complaints, then consider it your one-way ticket out of here."

"Yes, officer, we understand completely. You won't hear the slightest peep from us again. Oh, and would you mind signing this release form to appear on the show?" Mark asked, grabbing the clipboard from Ethan.

Max blinked his eyes in disbelief. "Leave. Now."

CHAPTER 15

*M*ax phoned Viv the next morning to fill her in on the previous evening's events.

"I couldn't find any evidence that Shauna or Vince Junior threw the bricks, so I had to let them go."

"What about the other note? Was it the same as the one from my house?" Viv inquired.

"Almost exactly. I had them both give a handwriting sample, and the results were inconclusive. Block letters are much more uniform in appearance than lowercase when trying to compare writing, so it makes it a challenge. I'm no handwriting expert, but neither of their samples looked to match the notes."

"Hmm… maybe the difficulty matching all-caps writing samples was taken into account by whoever wrote the notes," Viv theorized.

"Maybe, but their alibis seemed to check out and there were no witnesses, so I have no cause to charge either of them."

"And I wonder, though, why Vince Junior would be willing to put himself at risk with Sal by threatening his daughter," Viv mused. "I was kind of shocked at how he acted at the Giovannis yesterday. He must be pretty confident nothing will happen to him."

"Who knows? It could be a case of over-confidence and frankly, Vince doesn't seem to be the sharpest tool in the shed. So until more evidence presents itself, we're at a dead end here. When's the wedding?"

"Two weeks from today. I've never been so glad about a looming deadline in my entire life."

"Well, it seems that if someone is intent on sabotaging this wedding, two weeks is plenty of time for them to try to inflict more damage. We're going to keep up extra patrols, and don't leave the house at night by yourself," Max insisted.

"I'm not worried. Aggie will protect me if anyone tries anything."

A COUPLE OF DAYS LATER, Toni and Shauna arrived at Viv's office to discuss the seating charts for the rehearsal dinner and wedding reception.

"Thanks for taking the time to go over these seating arrangements again, Viv," Toni said. "It's so important to us that the wrong people don't sit at the same table. With our family, you never know what could happen! Hey, I meant to ask… the cop that arrested Erika and Vince Junior; that's your boyfriend, right?"

Viv looked around uneasily. "I wouldn't say boyfriend, exactly. We've known each other since high school when we used to date and have gone out a few times since I came back to town." She decided to leave out the part about Max dropping her for her best friend, not wishing to offend Shauna.

"Ah, I see," Toni said, arching an overly Botoxed eyebrow as best she could. "Well, Shauna says he's *quite* the looker. My advice is don't let him get away. Men will do almost anything to avoid getting married. My Shauna was certainly able to get her hooks into her Anthony, though!" Toni boasted.

Not wishing to speak any further about her personal life, Viv replied, "Noted. And to set things straight, Erika and Vince Junior weren't arrested. Max questioned them and didn't find enough evidence, so he let them go."

"Yes, I'm aware. Not to question his abilities, but I wonder if he tried hard enough? Because I just can't imagine who else it could've been," Toni tersely replied. "But it's just as well. We don't have a suitable replacement for Erika, and we must have the proper number of bridesmaids and groomsmen."

"Wait — Erika is still going to be the maid of honor, despite everything?" Viv asked in astonishment.

Shauna explained dejectedly, "Yeah, after finding out they weren't arrested, I asked Erika to swear she didn't do it and if she would still be in the wedding. I need her, and I know she's not gonna miss her chance to have as much screen time on the show as possible. Oh, Ma, show her the dress!"

"Viv, your suggestion to check out those dress boutiques in the city was spot on. Look at what we scored!" Toni exclaimed, eagerly showing Viv a photo on her phone.

In the picture, Shauna wore a sleeveless cocktail dress covered in white sequins and a daringly low neckline. The dress hugged her figure tightly, barely reaching past her hips and leaving little to the imagination. It was a far cry from the gown she had initially planned to wear.

"Wow," Viv said. "That's… something else."

"Doesn't she just look gorgeous? And so classy, like a model! I'm still not happy that Nonna Sophia's dress was ruined, but this one is a close second in my book and will be passed down to my granddaughter, God willing," Toni said with a wide grin.

THREE DAYS before the rehearsal dinner, Viv was out for an evening walk with Aggie, thinking about everything she still had left to do for the wedding. She dreaded the long week ahead with all the preparations likely to be combined with Toni's constant meddling.

As she contemplated the dazzling night sky, Viv felt a sense of calm wash over her. The sight of countless stars on the island still amazed her, a stark contrast to the starless city sky view she had been accustomed to. It was a humbling reminder of the immense expanse of the universe, making her troubles seem insignificant.

Aggie was busy sniffing around in the grass when Viv spotted a familiar-looking black SUV with dark-tinted windows driving slowly past them, stopping in the middle of the road. It was a moonless night and there were no streetlights on the small residential street, but Viv knew right away that it was the Giovannis' vehicle.

"Viv Vogel, what a coincidence running into you again!" their driver Richie called out. "We were just talking about you and some of this wedding business. Why don't you hop in and let us give you a ride?"

Trying to keep her composure, Viv replied, "That's

so nice of you, but we were just out enjoying the evening and headed back home. It's not far."

Richie paused for a few moments and then stepped out of the car with a malevolent grin. He wore black leather driving gloves and seemed burlier than she remembered. Aggie let out a low growl, her hackles rising. Ignoring Viv's refusal, Richie opened the rear door, revealing a person in the back seat.

Viv recognized him immediately from the photographs she found online. It was none other than Sal Giovanni.

"Viv," he said, smiling warmly. "I've heard you've been doing a great job with the wedding. Thanks for your professionalism. Why don't you take a seat in my car? There's plenty of room for your dog as well."

Even though she knew she had no choice, Viv tried to stall as Aggie whined and pulled at the leash in protest. Finally, Viv patted Aggie and said, "It's okay, Aggie. Come on, girl."

As soon as they were inside the car, the door locks clicked shut and they sped off into the night.

CHAPTER 16

Sal's cousin Tommy sat in the front passenger seat, whom Viv remembered from the night at the storage unit. "Hey Viv! Nice to see you again," he said cheerily.

"So Viv, sorry for this unusual way of meeting. Hope we didn't frighten you, but it's the best way for us to ensure privacy," Sal explained.

"Okay, what do you want to talk about?"

Like Uncle Gino, Viv was amazed by how ordinary and non-threatening Sal appeared in person. Rather than the expensive gangster-style suit she would've expected him to wear, he instead sported sharply pressed khakis and a pale lavender polo shirt. With his salt and pepper hair cropped neatly short and pudgy midsection, he seemed like a normal guy — like someone who wouldn't be out of place on a country club golf course.

"I hope that Shauna's not giving you too much trouble," Sal replied. "She can be a bit of a handful. I don't think she's ever been told no a single day in her life."

"Oh, Shauna's been a fine client. A little dramatic at times, but I understand. Getting married is stressful."

"What do you mean by dramatic? What are you trying to say?" Offended, Sal's affable demeanor abruptly changed.

"I, well, I mean…"

Sal cut Viv off, laughing. "I'm just joking with you! Dramatic is actually a very kind way to describe her." Sal then grew serious again and said, "Besides discussing my beautiful princess and her drama, I do have another reason for wishing to speak with you. I heard through the grapevine that you know Max Bennett, perhaps know him well?"

Viv didn't like where this conversation was heading. "Yes, I've known Max since high school."

"And now?"

"We are friends."

Sal turned to her, his blue eyes intense and unblinking. "Is there anything else?"

Viv frowned for a second, wondering if he was joking again. "No, I wouldn't say so. I mean, we see each other every so often and…" Viv trailed off, unsure how much information she wanted to give.

Sal studied her expression carefully, as if trying to pry into the corners of her mind. He smiled broadly, laughing softly to himself. Once more, his laughter dissipated, and he looked at her with an expression of seriousness that made her wish that the car's doors weren't locked, in case a hasty exit became necessary.

"So it seems you are rather close. Lucky man. In that case, there's something I need your help with."

Viv took a deep breath and answered calmly, "Okay, what is it?"

"I need you to pass along a message for me. I found out from a few of my sources that Deputy Sheriff Max Bennett from Harborside, Rhode Island, has been attempting to get information about some of my business affairs. Since I'm trying to stay out of the spotlight of law enforcement, I don't feel completely comfortable going to him directly. And I don't wish to be accused of making threats. So, I would like you to ask him to respectfully discontinue his investigation of me and my associates. Will you do that for me?"

Sal smiled at Viv expectantly, waiting for her reply.

"Yeah, sure. I guess I can do that."

"So, you guess you can, but will you?"

Viv felt every set of eyes in the car on her, waiting for her to say the right thing. "Yes. I will tell him to stop his investigation."

"Great! I knew I could count on you," Sal replied, gently patting her arm. "Now, one final thing. I heard that you ladies were figuring out the seating arrangements. Will you please make sure I'm seated as far away as possible from my uncle Gino? That man has been causing me nothing but headaches."

The car stopped where it had picked her up a few minutes earlier. Viv insisted that she didn't need to be dropped off at home.

"Now don't forget, dear, what we discussed. It was a pleasure meeting you," Sal said, shaking her hand.

Richie stepped out to open her door. "I… I won't. Nice to meet you, Mr. Giovanni."

The men waved goodbye, and the car quickly sped away to a vanishing point in the distance. Dazed, Viv started walking with Aggie, trying to process what had just happened.

. . .

Turning the corner, she spotted two people in a vacant lot on the opposite side of the street, looking around on the ground with a flashlight. Aggie barked as they got closer, and Viv stopped to assess the situation. The darkness made it difficult to make out any details. Both strangers abruptly looked up, startled by their presence.

"Viv! What on earth are you doing out here at this time of night?" Mark Simon asked, flustered, pointing the flashlight beam at her.

"I live around here. What's your excuse, Mark?"

"We were shooting some location footage earlier and then just before we left to head back, Ethan realized he didn't have his keys. So, we're retracing our steps."

"Oh, do you need any help?"

"Thanks love, but I think… ah ha! Found 'em!" Mark exclaimed, jingling some keys.

"Great, see you later."

"Hey, Viv! Don't forget about my invitation. We're only here for a few more days. Would hate to see you miss out on being featured on the show," Mark called out after her.

"Right. Okay, goodnight."

Once at home, Viv immediately called Max. "Max, I know it's late, but I need you to come over right away."

CHAPTER 17

After Max arrived, he sat speechless as Viv recounted the details of her unexpected car ride with Sal Giovanni.

"Did he make any threats toward you?" Max asked once she finished.

"No, there weren't any threats. In fact, he was adamant he didn't want to make threats. But I'd say they were most certainly implied."

"Well, I don't think there's much we can do right now from a legal standpoint since you got in the car willingly and weren't threatened or harmed."

"Max, that's not what I'm concerned about! You need to stop whatever investigation you have going on immediately. What did you do?"

"Nothing! I just made a couple of phone calls to some additional sources in law enforcement that Al pointed me toward. I didn't uncover anything beyond existing rumors, Sal's police record, or what was already mentioned in the press reports."

"What did you expect? Sal recently donated a two

million dollar training facility to the New Jersey state police. He's like Santa Claus to them. You think they'd give up dirt on him to a small-town deputy from the middle of nowhere?"

"Well, I would expect them to if they had any professional integrity. But I guess I'm just a dumb small-town cop."

"Hey, I didn't say that. It's just… I really care about you and couldn't forgive myself if anything happened," Viv replied, taking him by the hand.

"Babe, I promise nothing will happen to me. Why don't we try to forget about everything for tonight?"

THE NEXT MORNING, Viv headed over to the bakery to relay a full account of the previous night's goings-on to her sister. She waited for the place to clear out, then described her intimidating encounter with Sal Giovanni.

"Viv! Are you serious? That's crazy! Are you sure you're doing all right? Why didn't you call me right away?"

"I'm fine, Bets. And I had to call Max first, given he was the person they so-called weren't threatening. He came over to my place."

"Ah, I see," Betsy said, smiling.

"Oh, stop it now. Also, something else weird happened that I don't know how to explain. On my way back after they dropped me and Aggie off, I ran into Mark Simon and his assistant, Ethan. They were in that empty lot at Third and Elm, looking around with a flashlight, saying that Ethan lost his keys. Right after I asked if they needed help, they suddenly found them. Just seemed kind of odd, even for Mark."

"Hmm, who knows? Anyhow, I'm glad nothing horrible happened to you. Are you going to mention this run-in with Sal to Toni?"

"I probably shouldn't bother riling her up. Things are stressful enough already and the wedding is only a few days away. I just need to make it through the rehearsal and wedding. Then that will be the end of my dealings with the Giovannis."

No sooner had Viv uttered these words when she received a call from Toni.

"Oh jeez, speak of the devil. I guess I better take this. Hello?"

"Viv, I'm so glad you answered! I have a question for you. As you know, tonight is Shauna's bachelorette party in the city? Unfortunately, one of the girls can't make it. We'd really love it if you could take her place, seeing how the room is already booked and we can't get a refund."

"It's so nice of you to think of me Toni, but I'm not sure if I'm up for that much excitement tonight."

"Oh please Viv, don't be such a killjoy. Of course you should come, and Shauna absolutely insists on it! You don't wanna miss out on a crazy night!"

Viv exhaled in resignation. She didn't want to go, but wished to stay in Toni's good graces for the remaining time. Maybe it would make working with her easier.

"Sure, why not? I'll come tonight."

"Fantastic, hun! You won't regret it. We'll be by this afternoon to pick you up at two."

After Viv ended her call, Betsy gave Viv a quizzical look. "What was that all about?"

"They insist that I come to the bachelorette party,

but only because one of Shauna's friends canceled at the last minute."

"You seriously don't want to go to the party? I'd give anything to witness that madness. I'm sure it'll be like a live-action reality show!"

"Yeah, that's probably what they're aiming for, unfortunately. It's going to be filmed for *Monster Brides*, after all."

"Well, sis, it might help to think of yourself as an anthropologist, observing a tribe of suburban brats in their natural habitat."

"Hopefully some amusing antics are the worst issues I'll encounter tonight."

CHAPTER 18

By 7:00 p.m. Viv found herself at the Palm Court dining room inside the Plaza Hotel in Manhattan, where the evening's events were taking place. Surrounded by an excessive amount of potted palms in large planters, enormous marble columns capped in ornate gold, plush velvet seats, mirrored tabletops, and a huge backlit stained glass ceiling, the space oozed the kind of over-the-top extravagance that social strivers like the Giovannis couldn't get enough of.

Besides Shauna and Toni, there were fourteen other women, including Shauna's bridal party and a few select friends. Mark Simon and his crew were joining the group after dinner in the Grand Penthouse suite rented for the evening.

Shauna lorded over the raucous proceedings at the head of the table in the middle of the dining room, crowned with a gaudy rhinestone tiara and a pink satin sash slung across her chest emblazoned with "Bride to Be" — just in case anyone missed the memo on her importance.

Viv's attention was drawn to the occasional irritated looks they received from the more refined diners in the restaurant. Not to mention lecherous stares from men old enough to be most of the group's grandfathers.

Viv tried her best to remain inconspicuous while politely engaging in conversation. She found it really did help to think of herself as an anthropologist like her sister suggested, and the liberal amounts of booze being offered didn't hurt, either.

A couple of excited tween girls approached their table, giggling uncontrollably. One of them spoke up first, addressing Shauna directly. "Hey, aren't you Shauna Giovanni?"

Shauna nodded, her smile growing wider at the recognition she received as a BitKlip influencer.

"I told you it was her, Caitlyn!" the girl exclaimed teasingly to her friend.

"Well, do you two want a selfie with me or what?" Shauna generously offered to her young fans.

The girls eagerly agreed, and after taking their photos, scampered back to their table. "It's all part of the gig," Shauna explained nonchalantly, with a shrug.

As the dinner wound down, Toni rang her wineglass with a caviar spoon to get everyone's attention. "Alright girls, let's head up to our suite now for some cocktails and a special beauty presentation by yours truly, before the real celebration begins, ha!"

Erika had booked the evening's entertainment, rather than Viv. She hadn't inquired about the act but suspected it was likely to be male strippers, naturally.

. . .

UPON ENTERING the suite's living room, Viv spotted Mark and his crew already set up and waiting. As he watched the women file inside, Mark ogled them with a toothy grin and whispered something to Ethan, chuckling suggestively.

The suite was spacious and, like the restaurant, flamboyantly decorated. It featured a striking crystal chandelier in the middle of the room, and a large mirror with a gold-gilded border hung over the fireplace. The plush, powder-blue velvet sofa and armchairs had been moved out of the way to underneath the staircase leading to the suite's second bedroom upstairs. Rounded-back forest-green satin dining chairs were set up in a semi-circle in the middle of the room for the occasion.

Once they were all seated, Mark stood at the front of the room to address them.

"Ladies, it's a genuine pleasure to see you all here. Remember, everyone signed a waiver to appear on camera, ahem, I mean nearly everyone." He threw a testy glance toward Viv before continuing, "So please, just act natural and pretend we're not even here. And most importantly, remember to have fun! Now, let's get those drinks flowing!"

The room filled with chatter and giggles while Toni uncorked a bottle of vintage Veuve Clicquot and passed around glasses of the expensive champagne.

"Everyone, let's take a moment to toast my daughter, the lovely bride-to-be, Shauna! And of course, *Monster Brides.* Cheers!"

Toni placed her phone on a small tripod on a side table. "Just gonna live stream some of this on MyFace."

She grabbed a tray of ribbon-tied bright pink gift

bags adorned with the Lovely Lady Lashes logo and handed them out before starting her spiel.

"Good evening, ladies! I'd like to thank you all for coming tonight to celebrate the nuptials of our beautiful bride Shauna! As you can see, you've received a very nice gift bag containing an amazing assortment of samples from Lovely Lady Lashes, including their brand-new line of skincare products." Toni paused while her audience opened their bags with excitement.

"And if you'd like, you can order any full-size products from me too! For tonight only, I'm offering a fifteen percent discount on everything featured in the bag. And for all new representatives joining my downline, you'll get twenty percent off the two hundred dollar price of a premium starter kit!" Toni held up a small box Viv doubted was two hundred dollars worth of makeup.

"Huns, I'm telling you, this is a killer deal. This kit is an eight hundred dollar value and contains everything you need to start your own business with Triple L. And this goes for all you watching at home too!" Toni announced, directly toward her phone. "Okay, who wants to be my first demonstration model?"

Nearly every hand in the room shot up, the ladies shouting enthusiastically to be picked. Viv slunk down in her seat. She wondered if Mark would get paid by Lovely Lady Lashes for airing this infomercial, or if it would be edited out.

"Ashleigh, I think I saw your hand first. C'mon up here!"

With a squeal of excitement, Ashleigh bounded over to a chair facing the front of the room.

"Okay huns, first I'm going to show you the brand

new age-defying Miracle Mask. Made with all-natural ingredients, this mask will moisturize and detoxify even the driest, most tired skin."

While the rest of the group murmured in approval at these claims, on her third cocktail of the evening, Viv couldn't help herself.

"What toxins does it get rid of, exactly? Can it really do that?" she blurted out.

"Oh, you know, just regular toxins. The bad stuff that builds up in your body. The mask draws them out," Toni explained with a patient smile.

The rest of the group nodded in affirmation, some shooting Viv a pitiful look for doubting the product's efficacy in eliminating toxins. She felt pretty certain that toxins couldn't be removed from the body that way, but she chose to let it go.

"So, we're gonna apply this in a thick layer on Ashleigh's face and keep it there for about five minutes. It might sting a bit at first, but that just means it's working on drawing out the toxins," Toni explained, acknowledging Viv directly.

"Afterwards you'll see how beautiful and glowing Ashleigh's skin is! While we're waiting for the Miracle Mask to do its stuff, let me tell you about all the advantages of being a Lucky Lady Lashes representative. Of course, five minutes isn't enough time to go over all the benefits!"

"Ooh! This is really burning!" Ashleigh exclaimed. "Is it supposed to keep stinging like this?"

"Well hun, it might mean you have a lot of toxins in there to get rid of. No offense or anything. This stuff is made with one hundred percent all-natural ingredients, so you know it's safe," Toni explained authoritatively.

One of the other women shrieked and pointed at Ashleigh, whose face was turning visibly red through the mask.

"Please take it off!" Ashleigh shouted, fighting back tears. "Oh, it burns so badly!"

Flustered, Toni said, "Okay, I guess it's time to remove this. Apparently Ashleigh's skin is more sensitive than I realized."

Toni wiped off the mask and the crowd of women gasped when they saw the extent of Ashleigh's reaction to the product. Her face was bright scarlet, with large welts forming all over.

"Erika! Go grab a cold washcloth from the bathroom, will ya? C'mon hun, why don't you go lie down on the bed for a while with the cloth on your face. I'm sure it will calm down soon," Toni said, directing her victim toward the adjoining bedroom.

"I swear I've used this stuff a hundred times and have never seen this reaction before. I'm so sorry! Girls, I'm sure it's not the product, but don't use the Miracle Mask sample in your bags until we figure out what's going on with it. Okay, let's move on to the next demonstration. Can I get another volunteer?"

"Ma, please. I think we've all seen enough for now," Shauna snapped.

Toni smiled apologetically at her daughter and their company. "Okay, okay," she said ruefully. "I just thought you girls would want to see all the other wonderful Triple L products that definitely wouldn't have that type of reaction."

"Another time, Ma! Now, who needs another drink?"

Toni muttered under her breath as she collected her samples from the table and stopped the live stream on her phone. She approached Mark, who was talking excitedly with Ethan about the brilliant scene they had just captured for the show.

"Mark, can I ask that you please don't use what you just filmed? It could maybe look bad for my business, ya know what I mean?"

"Sorry, love, I can't make any promises. Just take a look at the contract you signed. You agreed that any footage you appear in could be used at our sole discretion. But, the show is only an hour long, and the night is young, so you never know. Still lots to capture for the episode, and we haven't even made it to the wedding yet!"

"Okay Mark, I understand. I just hope there's enough other footage for you to use instead."

"I will keep that in mind, love," Mark replied without assurance, turning back to Ethan.

"Shauna, why don't you open your gifts now?" Toni suggested, steering her daughter to a table overflowing with brightly wrapped presents.

An hour later, after Shauna had opened all her gifts and now had enough lingerie and other items to open her own adult-themed shop, there was a knock at the suite's door.

"Who could that be?" Erika asked, answering the door. "The police!" she exclaimed with mock concern.

A man dressed in a police officer's uniform entered the suite and approached Shauna.

"Shauna Giovanni, you're under arrest. For the crime of being sexyyy!"

On cue, two other men posing as police entered the room with a portable speaker blasting dance music. All three surrounded Shauna and started dancing and baring themselves down to their skimpy briefs. The ladies went wild, egging Shauna on. Toni stuffed wads of bills into their briefs and latched onto one of the dancers, shimmying with reckless abandon.

Viv stood alone against the wall watching the festivities, drinking her fourth, and vowed to be last, cocktail of the night. She tried hard not to blush, thinking of Max.

Mark noticed her standing there. "Don't you want to join in, love? I thought that law officers were just your type," he said tauntingly.

"No, I'm good," Viv replied, turning her back to him.

"Ah, Viv. I'm kidding! You know, it's none of my business, but I did find out from a former classmate of yours about how terrible Max treated you in high school. How he left you for your best friend and then married her, nonetheless! And I hate to break the news if you haven't already found out, but I'm afraid that this same person mentioned they heard that Max and his ex-wife might be getting back together. I'm sorry. If you were hoping for something more serious with him, it might be too late."

Blanching, Viv reeled toward Mark. "Who told you that!"

"Well, I'm afraid I can't divulge my source. But it sure sounded credible to me. Never forget, you deserve better, love."

"What, you?" Viv replied with disgust.

"Maybe, but I suppose it depends on what you're looking for. *I'm* certainly not the marrying type. Once was enough for me, along with the bloody alimony payments coming out of my account every month," he scoffed derisively.

"I wish you'd save your efforts for someone else," Viv responded, gesturing to the room of drunk and giggling women.

"No, not enough of a challenge there. You're a rare one, Viv Vogel," Mark replied, as she walked away to grab another drink.

Viv tried not to take what Mark said too seriously. *Max wouldn't keep that from me,* she told herself. But she still couldn't help entertaining the nagging feeling that Mark might be right.

At last, the strippers were gone, and the party was winding down. The film crew started packing up and the guests were leaving to go back to their rooms. Shauna was passed out cold on the couch. They were all supposed to meet in the hotel restaurant for brunch in the morning, and Viv decided it was a good time for her to return to her room as well.

"Mark, before you go, can you help me get Shauna to her bed?" Toni asked. "Poor thing had too much of a good time."

"Sure Toni, I'll help," he replied.

While they were putting Shauna to bed, Viv left without saying goodbye. In the hallway on the way to her room, she heard a familiar voice behind her.

"Going to bed so soon, love?"

"Yes Mark, I am, actually. I'm exhausted," Viv replied wearily. She reached the door to her room and dug through her bag for the keycard.

"That's too bad. The crew and I were going to hit

the bar for a nightcap and I thought you might want to join us."

Viv opened the door and turned around in the doorway, facing Mark. "Thanks, but I think I'll need to pass this time."

She was closer to him than ever before, prompting an overwhelming urge to shut the door in his face.

"Alright, if you change your mind, we'll be…"

Instead of slamming the door shut, Viv suddenly grabbed Mark by the shoulders and gave him a kiss that he eagerly returned. As he embraced her, Viv came to her senses and pushed him back into the hallway outside her room more forcefully than she meant to.

"This never happened! Understand?"

"I understand perfectly well, love-struck Viv Vogel! But our passionate encounter will continue soon enough!" Mark called out from the hallway, as Viv quickly shut the door.

Viv felt her heart racing. She wasn't sure what had just made her kiss Mark like that. Maybe partly she wanted to get revenge for what she found out about Max and Emily, even though she realized it was nothing more than a rumor and Mark was hardly a trustworthy source.

Thinking that she should get to the bottom of it, Viv picked up her phone to call Max, but stopped. She already did one irrational thing and didn't need to make it worse; it would be best to wait until tomorrow when she was sober.

CHAPTER 19

Sprawled on the bed in her silver vintage Giorgio Armani cocktail dress from the night before, Viv awoke to shouting outside her room and someone loudly knocking. Hazily, she recalled what happened with Mark, and her first thought was that he had returned from his night at the bar to come and harass her.

"Viv, Viv!" she heard Toni calling in a hoarse whisper. "Please open the door! Oh my gawd, Shauna lost her engagement ring!"

With a start, Viv looked at the bedside clock. It was already 10:00 a.m. and brunch was about to start in an hour. She meant to set her alarm for 9 o'clock, but forgot. Jumping out of bed, she rushed to open the door.

"Viv, hurry, slip your shoes on. You gotta come help me calm Shauna down!"

Stepping into the hallway, to Viv's horror, she saw Mark and his crew filming outside of Erika's room. Ignoring Mark's big smile and nod when he spotted her, she peered inside the room, which Shauna was well on her way to destroying.

"Where is it, I know you have it somewhere!" Shauna cried. She had thrown Erika's clothes all over the room and was proceeding to rip the bedding off.

"Shauna, you need to chill out! I didn't take your stupid ring — I don't know what you're talking about!" Erika yelled back at her.

"Somebody took it from me, and who else would want to but you!" Shauna shrieked even louder.

"Are you sure it's not in Shauna's room?" Viv quietly asked Toni.

"Yeah hun, we're sure. We looked all around every square inch of the room and suite."

"Do you mind if I go double-check?" Viv asked.

"Be my guest hun; the door is still open."

In the penthouse suite corridor, Viv passed a concerned-looking hotel staff member exiting the suite, followed by Ethan. Surveying Shauna's disheveled room, Viv spotted the enormous emerald-cut diamond ring in an open desk drawer, sparkling in the brilliant morning light streaming through the bay windows.

Grasping it in her hand with a sigh of relief, she made her way back to Erika's room, where Toni was busy berating a hotel employee.

"What do you mean, we have to leave? You told us check-out isn't until noon! Is our money no good here?"

Viv cleared her throat and held up the ring. "Shauna, I think this is what you're looking for? It was in a drawer in your room."

"What, seriously? We looked everywhere, including the drawers!" Shauna exclaimed, bounding over to Viv and yanking the ring away. She eyed Viv suspiciously and turned to Erika. "I know you had something to do with this!" Shauna sputtered with fury, pointing at Erika. "I don't know how, but I just know it was you!"

By now, the rest of the ladies from the bachelorette party were out of their rooms and gathered around to see what the commotion was all about, along with a few random hotel guests.

"Brunch is canceled, and it's time to leave!" Shauna declared.

"Yes, I think that's best for everyone," the harried staff member curtly remarked.

"Mind your own business!" Shauna threatened, as he left to attend to other matters. "This place is an overpriced dump anyways!"

"Okay, girls, let's pack up and get out of here before they call the cops. That's the last thing we need," Toni said. "Oh, and don't forget to stop by our suite for your free samples of my Healthful Living rejuvenation tonic. I was gonna give them out at brunch today. Just the perfect pick-me-up after a celebration like last night. Am I right, ladies?"

ONCE BACK AT HOME, Viv debated if she should confront Max now about what Mark revealed to her last night, or wait until the wedding was over, when things were less demanding. Fidgeting with the phone in her hand, she decided that it might be best to get it over with.

"Hey Viv, what's up? Are you still in the city?" Max asked.

"No, um, we left a little early. There was… an incident. It's a long story. I'll tell you later. I'm calling because I ran into Mark Simon last night and I need to ask you about something he mentioned."

"Okay, now I'm intrigued."

"He said he spoke with one of our former classmates recently, who told him they heard you and Emily might be getting back together. Is it true?"

Max paused for a second, taken aback by the accusation. "Viv, there's no truth to that whatsoever. You should know by now I wouldn't hide something like that from you. In fact, it's just the opposite. I'm fighting Emily to get more custody time with our daughter. Have you also thought Mark might not have heard any rumors at all and is just playing a game with you? I've noticed the looks he throws your way."

"I'm sorry if it sounds accusatory. I knew it probably wasn't true, but you can't blame me for being a little paranoid."

"I realize that my reputation precedes me, but there is nothing I can do about it other than try to prove to you that I'm different now and win your trust."

"I know. And I'm doing my best to let my guard down and let go of the past."

Feeling a pang of remorse over the memory of her kiss with Mark, Viv thought it might be best to fess up right now and tell the truth.

"Max, there's something you should know."

"Okay, what is it?"

At the last second she changed her mind, thinking it would hurt him more, rather than improve the situation.

"I uh… I trust you. I really do."

"Oh, well, I'm glad to hear! You had me nervous there for a second."

"Ha, didn't mean to scare you. Sorry, I need to go.

There are some details I still need to work on for the wedding rehearsal and dinner."

"Okay, babe, no problem. And Viv? I uh, trust you too."

Viv felt wracked with guilt. She knew she needed to tell Max what happened between her and Mark… eventually. She just had to make it through the Giovannis' wedding, first.

THE NEXT DAY, Viv was immersed in logistical coordination for that evening's wedding rehearsal and dinner, including the deliveries to the Masonic Hall and the restaurant for the dinner reception, Marco's Little Italy. Toni had been texting her all morning and was driving her crazy. Another one came in:

> Viv, make sure all the liquor going to the restaurant is stored away safely. K, thx!

There might be one less bottle if this keeps up, Viv thought to herself.

She headed over to the wedding venue to oversee the delivery and placement of the marble columns. Viv tried to arrange for all the day's deliveries to happen well before 12:30 a.m. when Toni and Shauna were due to arrive.

Viv scheduled the delivery of the columns from the prop company for 11:30 a.m., and they were now running late. She was getting nervous that they had possibly missed the ferry when she heard a loud truck pull up outside.

Meeting the delivery men at the door, Viv was

perplexed because they were carting in much smaller columns than what she had ordered.

"Hi there, I'm the wedding planner. I only ordered two ten-foot columns, not any extra smaller ones."

"Nope, not according to our order," one of the delivery men replied. "Says right here on the paperwork. Two three-foot columns, that's it."

"What do you mean, *that's it?* I know what I ordered. I have a copy right here," Viv insisted, reaching for her phone.

"Look lady, that's what you claim, but it's not what it says on our paperwork, and not what we brought. So, do you still want these?"

"What I want is what I ordered. Can you have those here by tomorrow morning?"

"Sorry, nothin' doin'. Those are specialty items from our New York warehouse. Takes at least four days to fill the order and deliver."

"Well, that's not going to help me; the wedding is in three days. Fine, we'll take the small columns. Place them up front where the tape is on the floor."

Just then, Toni and Shauna entered the venue. It was rare for them to be on time, let alone early.

"What's going on here? Is something wrong?" Toni asked with a scowl.

Viv sighed and steeled herself. "The marble columns. They're seven feet too short."

"Are you freaking kidding me!" Shauna yelled at the top of her lungs. "That was the one thing I asked you to make sure was right! How could you let this happen?" She started sobbing loudly.

"This is totally unacceptable!" Toni cried out, stamping her stiletto-heeled foot. "And say goodbye to your recommendations, Viv. One more screw-up and you are history! There, there baby," she cooed, hugging Shauna and wiping away her tears.

"Hey, I'll take responsibility when due, but I swear, I have the correct order right here," Viv replied, holding up her phone. "They brought the wrong size," she said, gesturing to the drivers, who were completely unfazed.

"Is that true?" Toni asked, turning her fury toward the delivery men.

"Like we already said, lady, it was on the paperwork. We just bring what we're told."

"Is that so? Ever heard the name Giovanni, hmm? I guess you don't realize who you're messing with. We'll never use your company for another event again or recommend you to anyone we know. In fact, I could probably have your business shut down. How would you like that?"

"Call the office then if you have a complaint. Don't matter none to me. Can you sign for the delivery? We ain't got all day," the other man replied, holding out the clipboard to Viv.

After the drivers left, Viv set about trying to rectify the situation with Toni and Shauna. "So, I was thinking, what if we turn these into candle pillars instead?" she offered. "I think they'll actually look pretty nice."

"Yeah, whatever," Shauna said gloomily.

"You're gonna make this right, and it better look great," Toni threatened. "I was going to ask if you wanted to join us for my Lovely Lady Lashes makeup demonstration with the girls, but it looks like you've got lots to do. You still might wanna think about my offer to sign up as a Triple L representative just in case this wedding planner thing doesn't work out for you."

Viv took a deep breath. "Sure," she replied, trying her best to stay composed.

"Alright then, tell the girls we're in the dressing room when they get here."

Viv was relieved she wouldn't have to endure Toni's tiresome sales pitch once again.

THE WEDDING REHEARSAL itself went much better than Viv anticipated. There was only one minor fight between Shauna and Erika, and everyone showed up mostly sober. At this point, however, Viv didn't congratulate herself too much; the hours-long rehearsal dinner was still next on the agenda.

The Giovannis decided to invite all their friends and family to the dinner and make it a huge pre-wedding party. Viv was already at Marco's Little Italy restaurant to get things set up.

With drab threadbare carpets and sun-faded photos on the walls, the old restaurant had seen better days, but the table decorations she had placed brightened things up a bit. Viv was studying the seating chart and putting the name placards on tables when she received a text from Max.

> I'm on duty tonight — hope everyone behaves themselves. Call me right away if anything happens.

Max was concerned about this large gathering of inebriated and feuding Giovannis all in one place. Viv already tried to reassure him that she could handle it and would be fine, but truthfully, she was a bit nervous herself. She was in the kitchen checking on how the food was coming along when Mark Simon appeared.

"Hi love, looking forward to the big day?"

"If you mean the day when you leave town, then yes. I'm certainly looking forward to it."

"Ha ha, what a kidder! I thought you did a bang-up job with the wedding rehearsal earlier — the ceremony is sure to be wonderful. Are you sure I can't convince you to change your mind about signing the release? I promise this is the last time I'll ask."

"Mark, I'm sure you know my answer by now. And I'm guessing you know my request in return?"

"Right. Don't worry, we'll keep out of the way, won't even know we're here," Mark replied dejectedly.

"Well, Viv, it really is too bad that you won't be appearing on the show. I predict this will be one of our highest-rated *Monster Brides* episodes yet. I want it to be the last show of the season, aired right before we start the new season of *Jersey Wives*. And I just asked Shauna to be our newest *Jersey Wives* cast member. It'll be the greatest character segue we've ever done! She's bound to generate fantastic ratings."

"Oh, good for her. I'm sure she'll be perfect for it. Now, do you mind? I'm sort of busy."

Toni arrived at the restaurant and approached Viv with an impatient huff. She had changed into a gold lamé cocktail gown with a long slit up the leg, much too formal for the occasion.

"Viv, did you make sure that the VIP table is front and center, and Uncle Gino's table is as far from ours as possible?"

"Yes, exactly like the seating chart showed, and as we discussed," Viv remarked. She tried to contain her annoyance, as she knew the night was just beginning and would need to pace herself.

"Fantastic. Not that I have anything against the guy, but he and Sal are still having a little family business dispute."

"Hey Viv! Did you hear about me being asked to join the cast of *Jersey Wives*?" Shauna asked, grinning excitedly.

"I did. Congratulations, Shauna. I'm sure you'll be a big hit."

Soon the guests began to filter in. "Alright, hun. Time to start with getting those drinks going," Toni ordered Viv.

Just then, Toni's cousin Lisa approached them. "Lisa, this is our fantastic wedding planner Viv I was telling you about. Well, she did have one screw-up, but it wasn't entirely her fault, so I'm willing to let it slide. Viv, this is my cousin Lisa," Toni explained.

"Hi Viv, nice to meet you," Lisa said, grabbing Viv's hand with a firm shake and subtle wink. As Toni left them to attend to other guests, Lisa leaned over and whispered encouragingly, "I know you got this. But let me know if you need any help with wrangling Toni tonight."

THE EVENING's festivities began with guests reveling in a lavish cocktail hour, ensuring they would be plenty merry and tipsy by dinner. The place was getting crowded, but everything seemed to be going according to plan until Erika started ranting at Shauna.

"You think you're so special now that you're gonna

be some big TV star! Those women on *Jersey Wives* are a bunch of dumb backstabbers!" Erika shouted.

"You're the dumb backstabber! Get out of here, now!" Shauna shrieked, throwing her glass of Dom Perignon in Erika's face.

Erika returned the favor by throwing what little was left in her glass at Shauna. "Gladly! Vince, let's go!" she cried, grabbing Vince Junior by the arm.

Mark stood on the sidelines, excitedly giving orders via headset to the crew.

"Oh, and just so you know," Erika said, turning dramatically as she reached the door. "Mark asked if I wanted to be a special recurring guest on *Jersey Wives*. I said I'd think about it."

Shauna glared over at Mark with daggers in her eyes and ran toward the ladies' room, with a couple of bridesmaids following after.

Fortunately, Shauna's antics didn't seem to faze anyone, and Viv laughed the whole episode off, even though she was dealing with a glass of spilled champagne and a petulant bride-to-be. Looking back, this would be a minor inconvenience for the night, as within the hour, Uncle Gino would be found collapsed on the floor.

CHAPTER 20

iv called 911 as soon as Gino was discovered. Max showed up shortly after — he heard the call for the paramedics go out over dispatch and arrived before the ambulance could manage to get there.

As the paramedics tended to Gino, Viv briefly explained to Max what led up to his collapse — the tension between Sal and Gino beforehand, and his last word, "soup."

Ten minutes after arriving, a paramedic pulled a sheet over Uncle Gino and shook his head. There was nothing more they could do for him.

Toni and a group of women consoled a sobbing Shauna. It was hard to tell if she was more upset about what happened to her great-uncle, or the fact that her party was now ruined. Viv observed Mark having an animated conversation with Ethan, while the crew continued to film the chaotic aftermath. Viv supposed that Mark would be ecstatic at this significant turn of events.

Noticing his presence, Sal fixed his eyes on Max, his gaze unblinking. Tommy stood next to Sal with a cigar in his mouth and arms crossed, wearing a fierce expression.

"So, I'm guessing from your uniform, you must be the sheriff around here?" Sal asked Max.

"Yes, I'm the Deputy Sheriff, Max Bennett."

The commotion of the crowd died away, and everyone watched their exchange with keen interest.

"Ah, given your apparent acquaintance with our mutual friend Viv, I thought it might be you. I heard you'd been making calls and inquiring about me, Mr. Bennett. Anything you'd like to ask me face to face?"

"Well, Mr. Giovanni, I appreciate the offer, but I'm afraid I don't have any questions for you right now. However, depending on the outcome of your uncle's autopsy, we'll see about that later. My condolences for your loss, by the way."

"Hmm… autopsy. Interesting. Fine, do your autopsy, but you're wasting your time. There's nothing suspicious or unordinary here."

"I hope the autopsy turns out to be unnecessary. But your uncle was no ordinary man."

"That we can agree on, Deputy. So, grab a drink and have some food. Enjoy yourself. That goes for everyone," Sal ordered. "It's what Uncle Gino would've wanted. Salut," he said, hoisting his drink in the air.

"Thank you, but I'm on duty and have work to do. I'll be in touch later if I have any questions for you."

Sal acknowledged Max with a curt nod before pivoting back to converse in hushed tones with his dutiful henchmen.

"Can we sit and talk for a minute? I want to find out everything you've observed tonight leading up to Gino's death," Max asked Viv.

"Sure. I just need to stick close by in case I'm needed for anything."

They found an empty table near the door and sat down.

"Okay, so what did you see before Gino collapsed?"

"Well, I noticed that Sal kept looking over at Gino while he was eating the soup. He seemed to be discussing something serious with the group of men he's with," Viv replied.

"You mentioned Sal and Gino got into a small exchange. What was that all about?" Max inquired.

"Uncle Gino asked Sal what he was looking at, and Sal told him, 'Be quiet and mind your own business.' Then Gino shouted, 'How dare you disrespect me,' and Sal laughed and said, 'Never mind, eat your soup, old man.'"

"That's interesting. I spoke with some of the people sitting with Gino, and they said he complained of not feeling well shortly after eating the soup, and then hurried to the men's room. So that was it? No other fights?"

"Earlier Shauna and her maid of honor, Erika, got into a shouting and drink-throwing match. Erika and Vince Junior left together afterward," Viv recalled.

"Hmm… and we know that Vince Junior happens to be loyal to Sal. They left before Gino collapsed? How much time passed between Shauna and Erika's fight and when Gino was found?"

"About half an hour or so. Do you think it's possible

Vince had something to do with it?" Viv asked with concern.

"If foul play was involved, he could be a suspect. Vince Junior had a lot to gain from Gino's death. With Gino out of the way, Sal would be in charge, and Vince might move up the ladder in the organization. Plus, this could ruin the wedding. You mentioned previously that Toni was so worried about what Vince might do that she wanted to hide a gun."

"That's one possibility. Or maybe Sal has grown impatient waiting to claim his share of the family fortune, or what if he suspected Gino had become an informant?" Viv theorized.

"I suppose it all remains to be seen. I need to call the Medical Examiner and get down to the hospital. In the meantime, I'm counting on you to be my eyes and ears for anything unusual."

"Of course. Let me know if you find anything out as well."

Mark's production had stopped filming, and Viv waited to approach him until he finished speaking with the crew. He seemed unnerved and his typically smug demeanor was gone.

"So, crazy evening, huh?" she said.

"Oh hey, Viv. Yeah, what a night. Earlier, Gino seemed fine, although maybe a bit drunk. I guess you never know."

"Yes, quite the turn of events. Fortunately for you, it should at least make for some good television, right? Or are you going to do the proper thing and not air it?"

"Well, 'good television' is a rather morbid way to put it. From a human interest perspective, though..." Mark trailed off.

"Ah, that's how you describe it. You know what I would call it?"

"What's that?"

"Tasteless."

"That's your opinion, love. We all have some less than glamorous aspects of our chosen professions."

"You can say that again," Viv replied, making her way to the kitchen.

Viv found Marco, the restaurant's owner and head chef, pulling a tray of bread out of the oven.

"Hey, Viv. What a horrible thing to happen, huh? That poor man. I feel terrible for the family."

"I agree. It's a very tragic situation and certainly not the happy occasion that I had planned for."

"Anyhow, Toni told us to resume the dinner service. Do you need something?" Marco asked.

"I was wondering if you noticed anyone messing around back here earlier, like with the food? The soup, specifically."

"No way! No one messes with my kitchen, I can assure you of that."

"Well, I'd like you to do me a big favor and take the soup off the menu for tonight."

"What are you trying to say? That *I* made Gino sick? That's quite an accusation you're making! Over twenty years, not a single person has gotten sick from my cooking," Marco insisted, crossing his arms with a frown.

"No, I'm not accusing you, Marco. I can't explain it right now. Will you please put the soup away in the walk-in and make sure no one else touches it for me?"

"Okay Viv, I'll do it for you. Only because your parents were some of my best customers."

"Great, thank you. Just hang on to it for a couple of days, okay?"

"Sure, sure. You're not gonna call the health department on me, are you?" Marco replied with a worried expression.

"No, I promise it's nothing like that. I appreciate it, Marco."

On her way out of the kitchen, Viv was stopped by Toni, who was dabbing her red eyes with a tissue.

"Viv, there you are! Can you believe this? Oh, poor Uncle Gino. And my poor baby, Shauna! We've promised her the wedding is still happening, no matter what. I asked Aunt Gladys not to have any services for Gino until after the wedding. Not that a funeral could even happen before then, given they want to do an *autopsy*," Toni said with a whisper. "Is there any way you can convince Max not to do it?"

"Toni, I would, but I don't think that's possible."

"And why does he want one done anyway, hmm? He's not gonna try and blame this on Sal, is he?" Toni asked with a glare.

"It's just a precaution. I don't think he believes that Sal had anything to do with Gino's death, or that it was necessarily foul play. But if this was intentional, Max needs to know."

"Well, he better be careful. I know for a fact it wasn't Sal, but if it was a planned murder, I couldn't imagine who it could be. Gino had a lot of enemies, and they're not all the greatest of people, if you know what I mean," Toni said with a knowing look.

"Anyway, most of the guests have left already, so why don't you go ahead and take the rest of the night off, hun? I can handle things from here."

"Okay, are you sure?"

"Yes, it's fine. The big day is almost here, so I bet you'll want to be up bright and early tomorrow to make everything perfect, right?"

151

CHAPTER 21

The next morning, Viv considered what had happened the night before. She felt certain that Uncle Gino's death was no accident, and it filled her with a cold dread. The wedding was in a couple of days, and she would feel much better if the culprit could be caught beforehand.

She decided to stroll down to The Book Nook, the only remaining bookstore in town. It would be a good way to get some fresh air and out of the house, plus she had a special order of books she needed to pick up.

Viv smiled in appreciation as she approached the bookstore. It was in a quaint, white clapboard two-story building at the top of the hill on Main Street. The living quarters on the second floor featured large windows framed by black shutters. On the bottom floor, two picture windows comprised of small panes showcased the latest titles. A welcoming golden light spilled out of the old wavy glass onto the sidewalk, brightening the gray and misty day. An arched solid oak door sat between the display windows, topped by an elaborate stained glass transom window.

Viv pushed down on the lever of the ornate wrought-iron door handle and creaked open the heavy door to the shop — inside it appeared deserted and smelled of old books and Earl Grey tea. The tightly packed floor-to-ceiling shelves sat lonely, waiting for customers to come and browse them.

A fat and content-looking orange tabby cat relaxed on one of the shelves. It stirred briefly and slowly blinked its eyes closed, paying no mind to Viv. Celia, the shop's owner for over thirty years, emerged from the back room.

"Oh hey Vivi, you made it just in time. I was getting ready to close up shop for the day. Let me go grab your order."

After retrieving the books for Viv, Celia asked, "So, how's the wedding planning business going these days?"

"Well, it could be better." Viv briefly recounted to Celia what had happened the night before at the rehearsal dinner.

"And even before last night, I can't say it's been the easiest event I've ever planned, with the reality show production constantly being in the way. And the bride desperately wants to be a reality star. It seems like being on camera brings out the worst in her."

"Oh dear, it all sounds awful! I read about that terrible tragedy in this morning's *Manitou Gazette*. The reality show you mentioned — is it the same one in town with the British TV personality?"

"Yes — that would be Mark Simon and he's been a major pain to deal with."

"Ah, I remember that fellow. He came here about a week ago saying he was interested in doing some mushroom hunting in the area and was looking for a book on the subject. He told me all about who he was and why he was in town. I wasn't familiar with him or his TV shows, but I heard about what he tried to pull in Audrey's shop — although I didn't mention it out of politeness, of course. He didn't exactly strike me as an outdoors guy, but I directed him to the plants and botany section and he bought a book."

"Hmm… I see."

"He wasn't the most likable fellow, if you ask me. He was rather arrogant and acted like I should have recognized him."

"Yep, that sounds like the Mark Simon I know, and he always behaves as if he's doing you a favor to talk to you."

"Call me old-fashioned and forgive me for saying so, but I'm not a fan of that reality television dreck. Personally, I feel between shows like that and social media, I've lost a good chunk of my customers," Celia replied resentfully.

"You're not the only one who dislikes his shows. And don't worry. You'll always have me as a customer."

"If only there were more like you, Vivi."

Walking back home, Viv suddenly had an idea. She searched her bag for Mark Simon's business card and grasped it, smiling.

LATER THAT NIGHT, she gave Mark a call.

"Hey Mark, it's Viv Vogel. Whatcha up to?"

Mark sighed dramatically into the phone. "Hello

there, Viv. What's prompted this intrusion into my otherwise peaceful evening?" he asked with an exasperated huff.

"Sooo… I was thinking. I might like to sign the waiver to appear on your show after all."

"Well then. What brings about this change of heart? I thought I was, oh how did you put it, tasteless? Or perhaps you think I'm vapid, or soulless, even?"

"I know, and I'm really sorry — the stress of the evening had gotten the best of me and I didn't mean to be so rude. But I thought about what you said about exposure, and that I might be letting go of a great opportunity. I don't want to miss out on my chance."

"I'm very glad to hear this, Viv. I knew you'd regret it if you declined. And I think you'd be perfect as the go-to wedding planner for the ladies' friends and families on *Jersey Wives* if you might be interested. So, do you want to make an appointment to meet tomorrow?" Mark asked excitedly.

"Actually, I was thinking tonight. Are you at your hotel?"

"Seriously? Lucky for you, love, I am. And I just happen to be alone tonight."

"It's not what you're imagining. I'll be busy tomorrow and want to get it out of the way. Especially before I change my mind."

"Well, I'm not going to deny a beautiful woman from visiting me, no matter the reason."

"Great. Meet you there in about half an hour?"

By 10:00 P.M., Viv knocked on the door of Mark's suite at the Seabreeze, the nicest resort on the island.

"Viv, you're here! Come in, love. Have a seat," Mark said, slurring his words a bit and motioning toward the sofa. He smelled strongly of booze.

Viv glanced around the room before sitting down. The suite was spacious, with a breathtaking ocean view visible through the sliding glass doors leading to a private balcony. Seafoam green walls and cream-colored furniture created an elegant and calming atmosphere in the room. A plush area rug in hues of blue and gold added a cozy feel to the luxurious setting.

A grand mahogany desk stood proudly in one corner of the room, covered in scattered papers and a vintage typewriter. The sofa Viv sank into was soft and inviting, adorned with silk cushions that matched the deep crimson of the curtains.

The suite was cluttered in the manner of someone who'd been living out of a small space for an extended time, but mostly neat, except for the multiple empty liquor bottles scattered about.

"So, I feel like we should celebrate with a drink for this momentous occasion. Can I get you something?" Mark eagerly asked.

"What do you have?"

"Well, let's see. This very excellent Scotch," Mark replied, holding up his tumbler. "Also, I have beer, and if you fancy wine, both Chardonnay and Merlot."

"Hmm... I'm sorry, I hate to be a terrible guest, but I only drink red wine, and Merlot gives me a headache. Would it be too much to ask for some Pinot Noir?" Viv asked with a flirtatious smile.

"Right then! Wouldn't want the lady getting a headache, would we? I can run to the bar downstairs and be back in no time. As nice as a place this is, no room service if you can believe it. I guess that's part of the so-called small-town charm. So while you wait, why don't you look this over?" Mark said, handing her the release form to appear on *Monster Brides*. "I'm sure you'll find everything is in order. It's all pro forma — shouldn't be any surprises."

"Great, thank you," Viv replied, flipping through the pages.

"Alright love, now don't go anywhere!"

As soon as Mark left, Viv reached for her phone and texted Betsy, who was sitting in the hotel bar.

He's on his way. Stall him if you can.

Viv had asked Betsy to come with her and hang out in the bar to delay Mark and let Viv know when he was on his way back to the room. She needed as much time as possible to search it for clues. Viv had an intuition that Mark Simon was hiding something, and she was hoping to find out just what it was.

She figured Mark would be back in about twenty minutes, depending on how long Betsy could keep him engaged in conversation. Viv wasn't sure if Betsy would be willing to go along with her scheme when asked, but she was thrilled to help out with this madcap adventure. At least it was more exciting than tending to the bakery or staying at home with the kids.

Viv started with the desk in the corner, stacked with an array of production notes, scripts, and random papers. She spent about ten minutes flipping through these items carefully, making sure everything stayed in place. Not finding anything of interest and realizing she was running out of time, she opened the bottom desk drawer.

There were more scattered papers; one caught her eye — a page from the Marco's Little Italy menu. Part of it was circled:

Classic Minestrone

Our house-made specialty is chock full of kidney beans, <u>mushrooms</u>, potatoes, carrots, zucchini, tomatoes, and pasta.

The word "mushrooms" was underlined in pen. *Odd,* she thought. Viv dug further into the crammed drawer, pulling out more bound production notes. Underneath, she found a small book buried at the bottom with the title *Wild Mushrooms of North America* on the cover. She picked up the guide and examined it. *This must be the book Celia was telling me about,* Viv thought. She opened it to a page bookmarked with a scrap of paper:

Coprinopsis atramentaria, also known as the common ink cap or inky cap, is a thin-fleshed and mild-tasting mushroom found throughout Europe and North America. While edible most of the time, it becomes poisonous when mixed with alcohol, giving it its other name: The Tippler's Bane.

It is commonly found in open areas throughout the spring and summer, particularly in meadows, pastures, and grasslands. It can also be located in urban areas and vacant lots.

Extreme illness may result after consuming inky caps and drinking alcohol, with reactions possible for up to several hours after consumption. Symptoms usually include nausea, vomiting, reddening face, feeling of agitation, palpitation of the heart, and tingling in limbs, and may arise five to ten minutes after consuming alcohol. Additionally, irregular, abnormal, and rapid heartbeat could occur, which, in rare cases, may be detrimental to susceptible individuals, with severe illness and possibly death occurring.

With a shock of realization, Viv immediately recalled the night she ran into Mark and Ethan in the vacant lot after Sal dropped her off. If they were hunting potentially poisonous mushrooms, their suspicious behavior made more sense now. She thought about Uncle Gino having some drinks at the party, eating the soup with possibly toxic mushrooms, and later collapsing.

Viv started to rip the page out of the book, but thought better of it and stuffed the entire volume into the bottom of her bag, along with the menu. She then received a text from Betsy:

> Stalled as long as I could. He's coming back.

Viv knew she had less than five minutes before Mark returned, so she began putting everything back in place. She quickly sat on the sofa, grabbed the waiver contract, and pretended to study it. A few seconds later she heard the keycard unlocking the door.

"Why didn't you tell me your sister was with you? You could've invited her up. Or perhaps you wanted me all to yourself?" Mark said wryly, setting down the bottle of Pinot Noir. "Hope this will do, love. They told me it's an excellent vintage."

"Well, it's Betsy's night to be without the kids and she wanted some time alone. So, you might not like to hear this, but I'm afraid I'll need to run this by my attorney," Viv said, holding up the waiver.

"What!" Mark exclaimed, laughing. "No one has done that, ever. If it makes you feel better, I suppose, but we're leaving in three days. What's wrong? You don't trust me, love?"

"Sorry, but I really need to get going."

"Wait! What about the wine? I thought you might want to stay for a bit, and maybe you know, resume where we left off the other night."

"Oh, are you not going to drink it?"

"Here, take it," Mark said in defeat, shoving the bottle toward her.

"Um, great. Thanks. I guess I'll be in touch soon, then."

"Yeah, yeah. Goodnight, Viv."

Once outside Mark's suite, Viv resisted the urge to run to her car. She texted Betsy back:

> Thanks sis. All clear. Found something very interesting. Will tell you later.

Viv locked her car door and immediately dialed Max's number. "Where are you? I have something that you need to see right away."

CHAPTER 22

*V*iv soon found herself at the Manitou County Hospital, where Max met her in the waiting area.

"Come with me so we can talk in private," Max said, leading Viv down the hall to a back stairwell.

A sign on the wall with an arrow said "County Morgue." The basement was poorly lit with a low ceiling, making it feel especially cramped and unwelcoming. Max gave Viv a seat on a wooden stool beside an old metal desk in a small supply room and shut the door.

"Okay, show me what you've got."

Viv produced the restaurant menu and mushroom hunting book from her bag, explaining how she found them in Mark's hotel room. She described the possible connection between the information in the guide about the inky cap mushrooms and Mark and Ethan searching the empty lot late at night, then a drunken Uncle Gino collapsing shortly after eating the minestrone at the restaurant.

Max listened intently, shaking his head. "I don't approve of your methods; this guy might be capable of anything. But I have to admit that you could be onto something — it just really worries me that you took matters into your own hands like that without talking to me first."

"I know, and I acknowledge your concern, but I had a hunch I couldn't ignore. I didn't want to wait."

Max sighed and nodded in agreement, then added, "Since this is potentially conclusive evidence we've got here, let's go pay a visit to the Medical Examiner."

Further down the hall, Max stopped at a partially closed door with a small window and knocked.

"Come in," a woman's voice called out.

Inside, a young woman with a blonde pixie cut sat behind a massive steel desk piled high with files and a mound of empty paper coffee cups.

"Oh, hey Max. What's up?"

"Hey Sally. This is Viv. She's found something interesting that could be related to the death of Gino Giovanni."

"Hi Viv, nice to meet you," Sally said warmly, extending her hand. "Sorry about the mess around here. Things have been crazy. This is the highest-profile suspicious death case the island has ever seen. Please, pull up a chair."

Viv presented to Sally the restaurant menu and the page on inky caps bookmarked in the mushrooms guide, briefly explaining her odd encounter with Mark in the empty lot. As Viv spoke, Sally raised her eyebrows with astonishment and jotted down some notes.

"Interesting. That's quite a story. I've never come across a potential mushroom poisoning before. I'll need to do some research on this inky cap species so I know what to look for when I run the blood tests. I should have the results by tomorrow morning."

"Thanks, I really appreciate it," Viv said.

"No, thank you for bringing this to me. It will make my job a lot easier if it pans out."

"But not mine if it turns out to be a poisoning," Max responded grimly.

"I suppose you'll have your work cut out for you, then. Thanks, you two. Max, I'll be in touch," Sally replied, getting back to searching through the stacks of papers on her desk.

"So, are you sure you're not upset about my covert operation?" Viv asked once they left the hospital.

"No, but I am worried about your safety. And maybe a little jealous about you visiting Mark Simon's room alone at night," Max said with a rueful smile.

"Max, you have nothing to worry about. But I do have something to tell you," Viv said, steadying herself with a deep breath. "After the bachelorette party the other night... I kissed Mark. That's all that happened and I completely regret it. I'm so sorry. I swear it meant nothing to me and it won't ever happen again."

A look of pain and disappointment crossed Max's face. "Oh, I see."

"It was just a drunken mistake on my part — I was overcome with jealousy and guess I wanted to get revenge because of the rumor that you and Emily were getting back together. Besides, the night was a disaster, and I ended up drinking way too much. I slammed the door shut on Mark immediately after I realized what I'd done if it makes you feel any better."

"It doesn't make me feel better, but I'm glad it didn't go any further. Viv, tell me the truth. Do you have any feelings for him?"

"No, absolutely not! Seriously, I completely loathe the guy. Nothing is going on between us now or ever again."

"Okay Viv, I believe you. And I hope you realize there is no truth whatsoever about me and Emily. Like I said, I wouldn't keep that a secret from you."

"I know, Max. My insecurities keep getting the better of me. Is there anything I can do to make this up to you?"

ALTHOUGH SHE WASN'T much of a cook, Viv made Max his favorite breakfast of French toast and bacon the next morning. It was a beautiful late summer day, and they decided to enjoy their food on Viv's sunporch. The garden phlox surrounding the porch was in bloom, the vibrant pink flowers emitting a sweet fragrance in the gentle breeze.

Max was discretely feeding bits of his overcooked bacon to Aggie under the table when his phone rang.

"Hey Sally, glad you called. Mind if I put you on speaker? I want Viv to hear this as well."

"Hi guys. So, I ran some blood tests on Mr. Giovanni. I found unusually high levels of aldehyde, which impeded his ability to metabolize ethanol, aka, alcohol. It's possible acute aldehyde poisoning led to atrial fibrillation, causing cardiac arrest. The build-up of aldehyde can occur when taking the drug disulfiram, also known as Antabuse, if mixed with alcohol. It's used to treat people with alcohol dependence and causes symptoms like severe nausea, vomiting, rapid breathing, weakness, dizziness, and headaches if taken before or after consuming alcohol."

"Wait, so you're saying it's possible Uncle Gino could've been taking a prescription for alcoholism and had a heart attack?" Max inquired.

"It's possible, but I can't know for sure solely with a blood test. His medical records will confirm if he was being treated for alcoholism or had a pre-existing heart condition. The thing is, though, this inky cap mushroom causes the same type of aldehyde poisoning and symptoms as Antabuse when mixed with alcohol. Is it possible to obtain any samples of whatever he ate during the party?"

"He only got as far as the soup, and fortunately, no one else ate it. I asked Marco, the restaurant's chef and owner, to stop serving it and save it," Viv responded.

"Great, I'll contact him and arrange to get a sample. Good work, Viv. I'll be in touch after I get the test results from the soup," Sally replied.

After Sally hung up, Viv groaned. "I'm so busy today, but I have to stop by Marco's restaurant and let him know about the sample request. He's very sensitive about his cooking. I don't want him thinking I called the authorities."

"Can I come with you? I'd like to ask him a couple of questions myself."

"Sure, why not?"

CHAPTER 23

Ohen Viv and Max arrived at his restaurant, Marco was in the kitchen prepping for that evening's dinner service.

"Oh look, it's Vivi and Deputy Max! What do I owe the honor?"

"Marco, do you remember the other night when I asked you to save the minestrone?"

"Yeah. So what now, you call the cops on me?" Marco asked Viv, only half joking.

"No. It's the Medical Examiner's office. They want a sample for testing."

"Medical Examiner! Ah, I knew it — they're gonna try to blame this death on me and shut down my entire life's work!"

"Marco, please, I promise. I can't give more details yet, but this has nothing to do with you."

Marco opened the door to the walk-in refrigerator with a sweeping gesture. "Well Viv, I hate to tell you this — it's not here. I told my sous chef the soup was no good and we needed to hang onto it. What do you know, though, he dumped it out anyway. That guy, he never listens."

"Oh, is it in the trash? They still might be able to get a sample," Viv commented.

"I'm afraid not. All five gallons, straight down the garbage disposal," Marco replied, shaking his head.

Max gave Viv a perplexed look and stepped forward.

"Look Marco, seeing how potential evidence has been, um, accidentally destroyed, I need you to answer some questions for me. What time did you start the soup preparations?" Max inquired.

"Well, it's not real minestrone if it's not simmering on the stove all day. I put it on at six a.m. and it was cooking until Gino Giovanni requested a bowl early that evening."

"Did anyone but you or your employees enter the kitchen the day of the rehearsal dinner that you're aware of?"

"Hmm… let's see. Well, Mark Simon and his crew arrived early to get set up. They wanted some behind-the-scenes shots and asked if they could film in the restaurant before the dinner started."

"Was Mark Simon left alone in the kitchen at any time?" Max asked.

"Yeah, I think he was in here for just a few minutes after his assistant asked me to come out into the dining room to read some paperwork they needed me to sign. Some kind of legal junk about agreeing to be filmed. Of course I signed it. Who wouldn't wanna be on TV? And Mark Simon, what a great guy! He even said how much he loved the restaurant."

"Okay, do you know of anyone else who doesn't

work here that may have been in the kitchen unsupervised?”

“Let me think. Oh, also Sal Giovanni.”

“Sal was alone in here? Do you recall under what circumstances?” Max asked.

“A delivery showed up before my kitchen crew arrived, and I was outside taking care of it. When I came back in, Sal was in the kitchen waiting for me. He wanted to make sure we had cannoli to serve with the coffee, since it wasn’t part of the original menu plan for the party. I mean, it’s Sal Giovanni. I’m not gonna say no to the guy!”

“How long was he alone in the kitchen for?”

“Oh, maybe two or three minutes, tops. Hey, I promise you, I have no idea what happened between him and his uncle, whatever it was. Please don’t tell them I said any of this! If they find out I talked to you — I mean, who knows what they might do.”

“Don’t worry, this is all completely confidential. Can you think of anyone else who was by themselves in the kitchen other than you or the staff?”

“That’s right, there was someone else while my crew was on break,” Marco said. “This guy who was the best man, and his girlfriend, the maid of honor. Vince Junior, I think he said his name was. I was in the walk-in for like maybe a minute and they were waiting for me as I came out.”

“What was their reason for being in here?”

“The gal wanted to know if there was any salad she could have instead of the main course; she said she was on a diet so she’d look nice at the wedding.”

“Hmm… okay, thanks, Marco. This is very valuable

information. I'll be in touch if I have any more questions," Max replied.

Viv sighed in defeat after leaving the restaurant. "Great, no evidence and multiple suspects. Is it possible that Vince Junior or Sal could have paid off Mark Simon to execute the plan? Do you think Sal would risk poisoning everyone just to hurt his uncle?"

"We can't rule it out. Sal may have calculated that was a risk he was willing to take. And there's still the possibility Uncle Gino had a bad reaction from taking medication, as Sally mentioned. I'll call and tell her the sample is a no-go, then see if I can gather any additional information," Max responded.

"Okay, be careful. I have some last-minute wedding stuff to attend to," Viv said, seeing three missed calls on her phone from Toni. Bracing herself for the worst, she gave Toni a call.

"Viv! Thank goodness you called me back! Do you have time to come over right now?" Toni asked in a panic.

"Yeah, sure. What's wrong?"

"You'll see when you get here."

Upon arriving at the Giovannis' vacation home, Toni led Viv into the living room, where Shauna was lying on the sofa with a damp cloth over her eyes.

"Hun, Viv's here. Let her see."

Shauna removed the cloth and sat up, making Viv gasp. Her eyes were blood red and swollen, with one eye nearly closed shut.

"What happened?" Viv asked, shocked.

"That stupid Lovely Lady Lashes mascara! The fibers must've gotten into my eyes from crying the other night!" Shauna exclaimed.

"We talked about this, Shauna. Don't you dare go around telling people it was from Lovely Lady Lashes. You were rubbing your eyes all night long!"

"Ma, everyone knows it's a dangerous product! There's even a lawsuit against the company right now for nearly blinding people. It's a scam!"

"Shauna Theresa, don't say that ever again! How many award cruises have you gone on with me thanks to Triple L, hmm? And all the parties and free stuff?"

"That doesn't count if you have to buy the product yourself, Ma," Shauna snapped back.

"Oh, the poor thing, she's so upset she doesn't know what she's saying. So, Viv, I wanted to see if you have a local recommendation for a good doctor. Maybe some prescription eye drops or something? I don't think even my makeup will help much with all the redness and swelling."

"If you ever think about getting that garbage makeup near me again, so help me!" Shauna cried, storming out of the room.

"Sure, I'll give you the number for Dr. Moore. She's great. Been my doctor since I was a kid," Viv said.

"Oh. She's that old? Well, I guess I'll take your word for it that she's good."

"Is that all you need for now, Toni?" Viv asked, trying to hide her exasperation. "I need to get over to the Masonic Hall and double-check everything is set for tomorrow."

"Sure hun. I'll make sure to call you later to see how things are going."

VIV WAS WRAPPING things up at the wedding venue when she received a call from Max.

"Hi Viv. Sally obtained Uncle Gino's medical records. There's nothing in there about him being treated for alcoholism, or having a heart condition. But if his bad reaction was due to medication, he could've received it from elsewhere besides his regular doctor. Or, there's still the possibility of intentional poisoning. I plan on giving our friend Mark Simon a call to see if he wouldn't mind stopping by the station for an interview. I need to make sure he doesn't try to weasel his way back to London before I can speak with him."

"Well, I hope something useful comes from that conversation," Viv replied.

"You're not the only one. So, how are things going with the last-minute wedding prep?"

"Shauna has some kind of eye infection from her mom's pyramid scheme makeup, but other than that, things could be worse. Hey, what are you doing later? I don't feel like staying home alone tonight."

"Ah, sorry, babe. I'd love to hang out with you, but I need to keep working this case. Plus, well… there's other stuff going on I can't talk to you about right now."

"Oh. Okay, I'll see you later, then."

Viv felt she needed to get out and take her mind off things to decompress before the big day tomorrow, so she texted Betsy.

Hey sis what are you up to tonight?

. . .

AFTER SPEAKING WITH VIV, Max checked his notebook for Mark Simon's phone number. It was time to bring him in for questioning regarding the inquiry into the death of Gino Giovanni.

"Yes?" Mark answered Max's call with a hint of irritation in his voice.

"Hey Mark, it's Max Bennett. I'm calling because we're still trying to fill in some gaps in our investigation of Gino Giovanni's death. I was hoping you could spare some time today to come down to the station and answer a few questions for me."

"Oh, hey there Max," Mark coolly replied. "I'd love to help you out, but unfortunately I'm in New York today for a meeting with some network bigwigs."

"Well, that's too bad. What about tomorrow?"

"We'll be busy filming at the Giovanni wedding tomorrow."

"Okay, what about after the wedding, then? If you have some free time, I'd be happy to meet you at the station tomorrow evening."

"Um, sure, Max," Mark replied with hesitation. "The reception might go late, though."

"That's no problem," Max assured him. "How does 9 o'clock sound?"

"Alright, I suppose I can duck out for a bit. I'll see you tomorrow."

"Oh, one other thing — can I get your assistant Ethan's phone number?"

$\mathcal{L}$ater that afternoon, Max observed Ethan in the sheriff's department's small interrogation room, behind the one-way window. In the room, the glass appeared opaque, but on the other side from inside a private office, Max could see everything.

Ethan sat alone, waiting for Max to arrive and begin their interview. His hands were fidgety, and his scrawny leg jiggled up and down as he stared blankly at the glass of water in front of him. With this apparent display of nervousness, Max hoped it was a sign Ethan would be more likely to give up what he knew.

As Max walked into the room, Ethan promptly rose to shake his hand.

"Hi Ethan, thanks for meeting with me today on such short notice. I'm Deputy Sheriff Max Bennett."

"Absolutely!" Ethan responded with enthusiasm. "I'm happy to help in any way possible." Despite his cheerful smile, there was a glint of hostility in his gaze.

Max settled into a chair and retrieved a small digital recorder from his satchel. "Do you mind if we record our discussion? My notes tend to be quite disorganized, and my memory is not as reliable as I'd like," Max admitted with a self-deprecating chuckle.

"That's fine," Ethan agreed in a less enthusiastic tone than before.

"Okay, great," Max replied, starting the recorder. "Just a reminder that you're here voluntarily and not under arrest. Got it?"

"Understood." Ethan lifted the glass of water, taking a long gulp.

"Let's begin by discussing your relationship with your employer, Mark Simon. How long have you known him?"

"We first met five years ago when I was in my second year at university. I applied for an internship at his production company and was overjoyed when I got the position."

"Why were you so excited about being an intern for Mr. Simon? Was it a well-paying opportunity?"

"No, it was an unpaid internship. But it held a lot of prestige and offered valuable experience. I've been a fan of Mark Simon's shows since childhood, and I still greatly admire him," Ethan answered matter-of-factly.

"What do you find so admirable about Mr. Simon?" Max queried.

"Well, I think that he's absolutely brilliant. He knows what makes people tick, and turns that into amazing entertainment for millions of viewers worldwide to enjoy."

"Alright, so you worked your way up in the company to be Mark's main production assistant. How long have you been in this role?"

"About four years now as head P.A. When I was an

intern, I was an assistant to his former production assistant. My tasks were mundane, like grabbing lunch and other errands, but I took every opportunity to learn and closely observed the P.A., hoping to one day take his place. Surprisingly, that day came sooner than expected when he had a disagreement with Mark and quit on the spot. Mark asked me to step in for him, and he was so impressed with my work that he offered me a job soon after. I gladly accepted and dropped out of university, much to my mum's disapproval."

"So, you must feel like you owe your success to Mark. I suspect you are very loyal to him, am I right?"

"I owe everything to Mark, and yes, I would do anything for him," Ethan replied emphatically.

"I wonder if that would mean possibly going to prison for manslaughter?" Max inquired, wasting no further time.

"What?" Ethan asked incredulously. "That pitiful old man who died at the rehearsal party? Why would we have anything to do with that?" he protested with a scoff.

"You might want to rethink your loyalty, given what we already know."

Max produced a book and a piece of paper from his satchel. "An associate found these in Mark Simon's hotel room."

Max opened the mushroom hunting guide to the page on the inky caps, sliding it and the restaurant menu across to Ethan.

Ethan briefly regarded these items with a scowl. "I know nothing about these," he replied with a steely gaze from his penetrating green eyes.

"Are you sure, Ethan? As you've probably heard,

American prison is no country club. I've already arranged with the county prosecutor that if you cooperate and tell us everything you know, you won't face the same fate as Mark Simon. Cover for him, and I can't make that same promise. Now's your chance to save yourself. Do you think he'd sacrifice himself for you?"

Ethan's confident facade wavered as he mulled over Max's proposition. Beads of sweat gathered on his forehead, betraying the unease that gnawed at him. He knew the gravity of the situation he was in, caught between loyalty to the man who had shaped his career and the looming threat of imprisonment. The silence in the room stretched taut, each passing second weighing heavily on Ethan's conscience.

"I... I don't know anything about what happened to that man," Ethan finally stammered, his voice cracking with uncertainty. His hands trembled as he pushed the items back toward Max, a feeble attempt to distance himself from the damning evidence.

Max fixed Ethan with a piercing gaze, his bright blue eyes sharp and unwavering. "Ethan, this is your chance to come clean. Mark Simon may have been your mentor, but you don't have to go down with him. Tell me everything you know about what happened at the rehearsal party."

Ethan's resolve faltered under the pressure, finally realizing he had no choice. After a tense moment of silence, he let out a defeated sigh and slumped back in his chair, his freckled face turning beet red.

"Alright, fine," Ethan relented, his voice barely above a whisper.

"You confess that the soup was contaminated with toxic mushrooms? Why did you do it?"

"We just wanted to make people ill. When eaten with alcohol, the inky caps can mimic food poisoning. Mark thought it would add excitement to the show. How were we supposed to know that an elderly man would have a fatal reaction?"

Max leaned back in his chair, absorbing Ethan's admission with a mix of disbelief and grim understanding. The pieces were slotting into place now, revealing a darker underbelly to the glamorous world of entertainment that Mark had carefully crafted.

He studied Ethan intently, noting the conflicting emotions that flickered across the young man's face — guilt, fear, and perhaps a glimmer of relief at finally unburdening himself.

"Did anyone else know about this plan? Who else was involved — did the Giovanni gang have anything to do with this?" Max pressed in an urgent tone.

Ethan hesitated, his eyes fixed on the table as if drawing strength from its worn surface. "No. It was just me and Mark... no one else knew. We thought it would be a harmless prank, an unconventional way to spice up the rehearsal party. I never wanted to hurt anyone," he confessed, his voice laced with regret.

"Putting toxic mushrooms into a soup is your idea of entertainment?" Max replied, incredulous. He couldn't fathom how callous one would have to be to endanger innocent lives for the sake of a twisted spectacle.

Ethan shifted uncomfortably in his seat, guilt etched across his features as he avoided Max's gaze.

"Mark was the one who came up with the plan and I

helped him find the mushrooms. On the day of the rehearsal party, he instructed me to get Marco out of the kitchen to sign the release form while he put the mushrooms into the soup. I was just following orders," Ethan insisted, attempting to justify his involvement in the crime.

Max regarded Ethan with a mixture of pity and disdain. It was clear that the young man had been manipulated and led astray by his idol, Mark Simon.

"Following orders is no excuse for such a heinous act, Ethan," Max stated firmly. "But your willingness to come clean and cooperate will work in your favor. I have a feeling that this isn't the only staged disaster that took place during this production, especially given some of the other unfortunate incidents that have happened. For instance, what about the bricks with the threatening notes attached?"

Ethan sighed and looked down with embarrassment. "Yes, that was us," he answered timidly. "Mark had me drive by and throw them at Shauna and Viv's houses. He wanted to stir up drama by making Shauna think Vince Junior and Erika were behind it."

Max leaned forward, consulting his notebook on the table. "Interesting. I had a feeling that was the case. There were also the incidents of the cut-up wedding dress and the missing engagement ring, where Erika was again the prime suspect. Were these also ploys to 'stir up the drama,' as you put it?"

Ethan paused, taking a sip of water before admitting, "You are right again, Deputy. The day we arrived to film Shauna trying on her re-fitted wedding gown at home, Mark had me sneak a pair of scissors upstairs while I was setting up the room for production. He told me to find the dress in the wardrobe and cut it up, while he stayed downstairs and distracted Toni and Shauna."

"And the missing engagement ring? Viv mentioned she observed you leaving the hotel suite before she entered, where she found the ring sitting in plain sight."

"I didn't take the ring; it was Mark. The night before, when Shauna had passed out and he helped Toni get her to bed, he slipped it off her finger. It was a spur-of-the-moment decision and too good for him to pass up. Later on, he asked me to replace the ring once we had filmed Shauna's meltdown accusing Erika."

Max frowned and asked, "So, do you find these stunts enjoyable? Messing with people?"

With a heavy sigh, Ethan replied, "Look Deputy, it's all part of the show. I'm not proud of it, but it's simply how we do things. Ratings were going down and Mark increasingly came up with ideas to make things more interesting, so to speak. He recently had done the same for some other productions back home in the U.K. with fantastic results. But presently there's an inquiry into some tricks gone wrong, unfortunately," Ethan admitted.

"Ah, the ratings — of course. My suggestion to you is to find another line of work after this," Max said with a disapproving look.

"And what about the mishaps with Toni's beauty products; did you sabotage those also?"

"Oh no, that wasn't done by us," Ethan insisted. "From what I understand, Lovely Lady Lashes products are total rubbish."

"Great, I have all the information I need for now and will handle things from here. Thank you for being open and honest with me today, Ethan. Your cooperation has been crucial in solving this case. We'll be in touch soon," Max responded, standing to escort Ethan out.

Ethan shifted nervously, again making it clear to Max that he admired Mark but was not willing to sacrifice his freedom for him. He turned and asked if Mark would know that he was the one who had informed on him.

"It's unlikely we'll be able to keep your identity a secret, so yes, I believe Mark will figure it out. But given the gravity of his actions, I doubt you'll need to worry about any retaliation from him for quite some time."

CHAPTER 25

The following morning, Viv awoke from the night out with her sister, blinking against the bright sunlight streaming into her room. She forgot to close the curtains before bed — the searing light felt like it was drilling holes into her eyes. Her head pounding, she put a pillow over her face with a groan. She had a vague feeling like there was something she had to do today, something important she was forgetting…

Then it suddenly dawned on her — today was the Giovannis' wedding! With a jolt, she reached to grab her phone. 9:15. She was supposed to have been at the Masonic Hall fifteen minutes ago to receive the flowers delivery. Her phone showed two missed calls.

She didn't mean to drink so much last night, but Betsy was the designated driver, practically egging her on to have more. Plus, she was feeling unsettled about what Max meant by saying there were circumstances he didn't want to talk to her about. Was he having second thoughts about returning to Emily after Viv revealed what had happened between her and Mark? Did it affect him more than he let on?

The missed calls were from the florist's delivery driver, with a message that they had left the flowers in front of the venue's doors.

DESPITE HER TERRIBLE HANGOVER, Viv sprang into action and arrived there within half an hour. The flower arrangements were outside, untouched, and she busied herself with hauling them in and putting them in place by herself. She wished she could go back home and sleep off her hangover for a while, but had to stay for the cake delivery and the all-important chocolate fountain for the reception in the attached banquet hall.

Toni and Shauna arrived by noon to allow plenty of time for getting dressed and taking photos before the ceremony at four o'clock.

"Viv, these flowers look amazing! Although do you think all the yellow is a bit much? Oh well, I guess we'll have to live with it. Hey, are you okay? You really look terrible!" Toni commented, not so helpfully.

"I'll be fine. I just went a little overboard last night, is all."

"I'll say! Do you want to try some Healthful Living herbal rejuvenation tonic? I have some samples in my bag. It works wonders, hun!"

Viv suppressed a wave of nausea, imagining what that stuff tasted like. "No thanks, I have some tea right here."

"In fact, I think I'm done with Lovely Lady Lashes to focus more on selling Healthful Living products. It's a much better company, in my opinion," Toni declared.

Shauna giggled and held up her phone. "Ha, she only says that now. Because of her epic fail during the live stream at the bachelorette party, Ma became a meme on BitKlip and MyFace, and not in a good way!"

She showed Viv some of the social media images mocking Toni and Lovely Lady Lashes. More than a few compared her to the *Jersey Wives* villain, Angie Greyson.

Toni let out a groan. "All thanks to Triple L, I guess my time on MyFace is over — it was good while it lasted. I don't know how I'm gonna make any money selling Healthful Living products now, but I'll figure something out. Why is it so hard for me to keep my reputation?" she asked, exasperated.

Shauna chuckled at this last statement of her mom's and shook her head. "Well Ma, I can't say that I'm sorry you're not gonna be on MyFace constantly — you were actually much nicer before all this started!"

"And I might say the same for you, always scrolling through BitKlip! Remember how much fun we used to have doing things together? We used to laugh all the time! Now it's just not like that anymore… it's like we're always arguing or something."

"Well, I'm not going to abandon my followers. But I tell you what, I'll only post my videos on BitKlip and not spend any extra time on there — if you stay off of MyFace."

"Okay, hun. Let's make a deal. If we can both hold up our part of the bargain, we'll go on vacation together somewhere nice this winter."

"Sure, Ma. Deal."

"And Viv, thanks for the doctor recommendation. She prescribed some steroid cream and eye drops. Shauna looks much better, don't ya think?" Toni asked.

Shauna was already made up, her hair artfully pinned in a tasteful updo. Her eyes were still quite red and puffy, and the caked-on makeup didn't do much to help, but she was remarkably improved from how she appeared the day before.

"Yes, quite a fast recovery," Viv commented.

"Okay hun, we'll be in the dressing area. The girls and guys should be getting here soon. And Mark Simon too, of course."

Viv was speaking with the photographer when Mark and his crew arrived a short time later.

"Viv! Everything looks wonderful. Amazing job, love. By the way, did your attorney have a chance to review the waiver?" Mark asked with a smirk.

"Yeah, about that — I'm afraid I won't be appearing on the show after all."

"Well, that's too bad. I suppose we'll have to get along without you. Anyhow, I know Max was just itching to talk to me yesterday regarding his investigation. He didn't mention exactly why he needed to speak with me so urgently, but I agreed to chat with him after the ceremony. You wouldn't happen to know why he called me, would you?" Mark asked, trying to sound nonchalant.

"Sorry, I have no idea. I guess you'll find out later?"

By 3:00 p.m. some early guests were arriving, and the hired string quartet began warming up. Viv received a text from Max:

Hi Viv, is Mark Simon there

Yes

Ok, see you before 4:00

Shauna and Anthony insisted on a playlist of their favorite 1980s power ballads for the ceremony, and by 3:30 the quartet began their performance with "Is This Love" by Whitesnake.

Suddenly, a cacophony of murmurs traveled through the crowd of guests. Viv turned to follow where everyone was looking and saw Max determinedly marching down the aisle in his deputy's uniform with another officer in tow.

Spotting Viv, Max approached and asked, "Viv, where's Mark Simon?"

"He's with the crew in Shauna's dressing room. She's having a last-second freakout since the zipper busted on her dress and needs to be pinned."

"Perfect. Being out of sight should cause less of a fuss in front of the guests. Show me the way?"

Mark was watching the chaotic scene of Shauna yelling at Erika as she tried to pin her dress together, when he noticed Viv advancing toward the open dressing room door with Max and the other officer.

Seeing them, Shauna stopped screaming, frustrating Mark. Ethan glanced around the room nervously and exhaled in resignation.

"Deputy, it's not that I'm not glad to see you, but you're a bit early for our meeting. We're in the middle of filming, as I'm sure you can see," Mark snapped irately.

"Not for long, I'm afraid," Max replied, motioning to the officer behind him. "Mark Simon, you're under arrest for the poisoning death of Gino Giovanni. Officer Lowell, please proceed."

The officer stepped forward with handcuffs out, reciting the Miranda warning to Mark.

"What! Wait, is this some kind of joke? Who put you up to this!" Mark exclaimed in disbelief.

"Hey, what are you doing? You can't arrest him! What about my show!" Shauna howled.

Toni grabbed Viv by the arm, gripping hard. "Make him stop," she hissed. "You can't do this!" Toni screeched at Max.

"What am I supposed to do about it?" Viv retorted, pulling her arm away from Toni's iron clutch.

"Sorry it had to happen like this, but we have an arrest warrant and the evidence is clear. He'll be given due process and have his day in court. Now please, make way. And you all will need to leave the premises as well," Max said, motioning to the crew, including Ethan.

Officer Lowell led Mark out of the room, hands cuffed behind his back.

"Nooo! My show, my show!" Shauna whimpered.

"Don't worry, love, it's still going to air. Especially with this evidence of my wrongful arrest!" Mark exclaimed.

Guests gasped in disbelief and excitement as Mark paraded through the venue's main room in handcuffs, followed by his production crew. The commotion nearly drowned out the quartet's version of Poison's "Every Rose Has Its Thorn."

Sal Giovanni eyed the scene with contempt. "Can you believe the cops at my daughter's wedding? The nerve of these guys!"

. . .

Officer Lowell escorted Mark to the police station, while Max stayed and took a seat in the back of the hall.

"I just want to make sure everything stays calm here," Max explained to Viv.

A few last-minute guests arrived and squeezed into some open spots near Max.

"Are you going to tell me what that was all about?" Viv asked in a hushed voice. She was a bit irked at the disruption Mark's unexpected arrest had caused right before the ceremony.

Max proceeded to explain the riveting details of Ethan's confession.

"Wow." Viv leaned back in her seat, stunned. "And what about the issues Toni's products caused at the bachelorette party and with Shauna yesterday — was that their doing as well?" Viv inquired.

"No. Apparently, the problems with the Lovely Lady Lashes products were the only disasters Mark and Ethan didn't cause."

"Huh. Well, I'm glad I never took up Toni's offer to buy any of that junk from her. So why did Mark do all these terrible things?"

"Ethan said Mark wanted to create as much drama and chaos as possible in order to boost *Monster Brides'* slumping ratings. In fact, he's been accused of further dangerous and illegal stunts on some of his other shows, and there's already a pending case against him in Britain, as we speak."

"It's not very shocking that he's performed such horrible acts before. What's going to happen to Ethan?"

"I convinced the prosecutor not to arrest him since he was so cooperative. He'll be deported and never allowed to enter the country again. And the same with the rest of the crew, whom Ethan claims weren't involved. So, kudos to you. Otherwise, Uncle Gino's death could've been chalked up to natural causes."

"Well, my already low opinion of Mark Simon certainly didn't hurt my suspicions. Oh, I need to go," Viv said, peeking at her watch. "You can figure out how you want to thank me later."

With the wedding due to start in just a few minutes, Viv made her way back to the dressing room to check on Shauna. Erika and a couple of the bridesmaids were trying to comfort Shauna, giving her tissues and attempting to fix her hair and makeup.

Toni turned her fury toward Viv, poking a trembling finger in her face. "You! What did you know about this?"

"Toni, I swear I didn't know Max was coming to arrest Mark. If I did, I would've asked him to at least wait until after the wedding."

"If I find out you're lying, just you wait. And you can forget about that promised bonus for a flawless ceremony! Okay girls, why don't you go ahead and gather in the vestibule. Viv, go tell the guys it's time. Shauna will be ready soon."

Now that the wedding party was all set and waiting outside the ceremony room, Viv left to give the string quartet their cue. The groom, Anthony, shuffled around nervously, looking pale and ill as if he were having second thoughts about his impending lifetime commitment to Shauna.

Toni reached out and patted him on the arm. "You okay, hun?"

"Yeah, I'm fine. Last minute nerves I guess."

The quartet started playing Bon Jovi's "Livin' on a Prayer," the signal for the wedding procession to begin.

Wearing a figure-hugging silver-beaded evening gown fit for a night at the Oscars, Toni escorted Ruffles, the ring-bearing dog, down the aisle. Ruffles was outfitted in the promised crystal collar with matching leash, along with a yellow tulle gown and a tiny pink satin ring pillow tied around her midsection. Toni proudly lifted her so Anthony could retrieve the rings, then took her seat in the front row, waving at guests like royalty.

Viv went to grab Shauna from the dressing room and found her staring blankly in the mirror.

"I can't believe Mark is gonna miss filming my walk down the aisle. You swear you didn't know he was getting arrested?"

"I promise you, I had no idea this was going to happen."

"Well, they'll have to let him go. Why would Mark have anything to do with Uncle Gino's death?"

"Shauna, are you about ready? It's time."

CHAPTER 26

*S*oon Shauna was on Sal's arm, striding down the aisle to the "Wedding March," the only traditional song chosen for the day.

Anthony's anxiety was evident as his bride approached; sweat ran down his face, and he nervously glanced around the room. Sal patted on him the back and whispered words of encouragement, taking his seat next to Toni, who was beaming with pride.

"Ladies and gentlemen, we are gathered here today…" the priest began, interrupted when the four members of the late-arriving group sitting near Max jumped to their feet. Max quickly moved to block the doors leading to the vestibule.

"Freeze! FBI!" one of them shouted, pointing at Sal. "Salvatore Giovanni, you're under arrest for felony racketeering and wire fraud. Hands behind your back!" he ordered, while another agent grabbed Sal, placing him in handcuffs.

They also rounded up Cousin Tommy, New Jersey State Senator Frank Murray, and two more of Sal's associates. Another agent went to the front and cuffed Anthony.

Mass pandemonium erupted, and the loudest voice belonged to Shauna. "Get your hands off of my father! Anthony, Dad, what is this?"

Toni desperately pulled on the agent's arm holding Sal. "What do you think you're doing? You're making a big mistake!" she threatened impotently.

Viv couldn't believe that the wedding she had undergone such great pains to organize had devolved into utter chaos. She peered over at Max, but he was staring straight ahead, averting her gaze. She realized that his prior comment about an unsharable secret likely referred to this.

The agents led the handcuffed men outside, where an unmarked white van sat waiting.

Shauna ran after Anthony, sobbing. "How are we going to get married now? I can't be a cast member on *Jersey Wives* if I'm not married!"

"Babe, I'll be out soon, I promise. We can always get married in prison, too."

"Nooo! How can this happen to *me?* It's not fair!" Shauna wailed. Max held her back as they loaded Anthony into the van.

Erika surveyed the tumultuous scene with a smug grin, while Vince Junior stood in shock with his mouth hanging open. Somehow, he had managed to escape arrest.

"What are you smiling at?" Shauna snapped at Erika. "I bet you two had something to do with this. Just wait, you'll get what's coming to you!"

"Don't worry, Shauna. Maybe you can be on *Celebrity Prison Wives* instead?" Erika retorted.

"Okay, everyone," Max said, addressing the remaining crowd of spectators. "The wedding is over. Time to leave."

Seething with rage, Toni turned to Max. "And what about our reception? All the food and liquor we paid for! The crystal and china? The chocolate fountain! What about that?"

"Sorry ma'am, but everyone needs to go now. You can arrange to come and retrieve any of your possessions tomorrow."

"Get your stuff, we're leaving!" Toni ordered Shauna. "The sooner we can get out of this dump of a town, the better. And I'll deal with *you* later," she warned Viv with a vicious glare.

WITH THE LAST guests slipping out the door, along with the FBI agents, Viv and Max were finally alone. Viv faced Max, her cheeks burning with exasperation.

"Look, I'm sorry you had to find out this way," Max tried to explain. "I would've told you if I could."

"When did you learn that the FBI was planning this raid?"

"Oh, about two months ago," Max replied with a wince, wilting under Viv's fierce gaze.

"Two months! If I'd known we weren't even going to make it to the reception, I would've put a lot less effort into it," she muttered in defeated disbelief.

"But that was actually the most important part. To make everything surrounding the wedding seem as real as possible. And the unexpected death of Gino Giovanni suddenly put the whole operation in danger. It meant the possibility of the wedding getting called off, and most of those scumbags would still be roaming around free for who knows how long."

"Real? What do you mean by *real?* You mean everything — the whole thing, was a set-up?"

Max cringed at the question and continued with a sigh. "I'm sorry to say that it was. A couple of months ago, the FBI got in touch to let me know about their planned raid and said they could use my assistance. They knew you were hired by the Giovannis and somehow knew we were dating, and thought that I could give them valuable intel," Max said, pausing.

"Please, go on," Viv replied, crossing her arms with growing agitation.

"It all started late last year when Anthony was picked up by the FBI and brought in for questioning. He was threatened with a long prison sentence unless he provided information about the Giovanni clan and associates. Since Anthony was dating Sal's daughter, they came up with the fake wedding idea so they could arrest and charge the gang all at once. This reduced the risk of arresting them all individually. In exchange for proposing to Shauna and going along with the sham wedding, Anthony would receive only a year in prison, instead of ten or more."

Viv sat back and buried her face in her hands. She thought about all the effort for nothing, and what she put up with throughout the whole ordeal. For a second she thought she might cry, but instead, burst into a fit of uncontrollable laughter. This was all so absurd, and she found it to be absolutely hysterical.

"Viv, are you okay?" Max asked with concern.

"I'm... fine," Viv managed to say between fits of laughter and tears in her eyes. It felt like ages since she had laughed this hard. "I'm just glad it's finally all over."

"And one last thing. You were right — the family was using the wedding as an excuse to launder money by buying expensive items through you and then reselling or returning them. You'll probably be asked to pass along records of all the financial transactions related to the wedding to the feds, in addition to any remaining funds. Minus your commission, of course."

"That won't be a problem. The Giovannis had me spend nearly every last cent of the money wired to me, anyway."

"I do have one small way to help make this up to you, I hope."

Max produced some folded papers from his jacket and handed them to Viv.

"What's this?"

"Tickets and an itinerary. For the sake of appearances, Anthony had to purchase a honeymoon vacation package, paid for out of his own pocket. A ten-day trip to Saint Lucia in the Caribbean, on a private jet direct from the airfield here on the island. Shauna wouldn't accept a cheap vacation. And he had to book it for real since it was very possible that Shauna would check on the accommodations and other details beforehand. Knowing that he'd be in prison instead of going on a honeymoon, the FBI made Anthony hand it over."

"And?" Viv asked expectantly.

"They offered me the trip as a thank-you for helping them out since it would otherwise go to waste. So, what do you think? Join me on a private jet to the Caribbean early tomorrow morning?"

Viv gave Max a mischievous grin. "I'll only go on one condition. Can I ask you a huge favor?"

At 7:00 a.m. the next morning, Viv found herself on a small private plane, waiting to leave from the airfield on Manitou Island.

Aggie sat next to her with her head resting in Viv's lap. Betsy was stretched out along the seats across the aisle, looking over their vacation itinerary.

Once they were airborne, Betsy remarked, "Wow, I still can't believe Max let me take his place on this trip. He must really love you."

Viv leaned against the window, gazing at the sunrise as the plane ascended higher and banked a turn over the island. The sea sparkled like gold beneath the brilliant glow of the morning sun.

"I know he does," she said, smiling. "I know."

ABOUT THE AUTHOR

C.J. Lee lives in the Pacific Northwest, where she enjoys going on long walks in nature, thinking of new ideas for stories. *RSVP for Murder: A Viv Vogel, Wedding Planner Cozy Mystery,* is her first novel.

Visit authorcjlee.com for more information.